My Buddy,
THE KING

Also by Bill Brittain

All the Money in the World
Devil's Donkey
The Wish Giver: Three Tales of Coven Tree
Who Knew There'd Be Ghosts?
Dr. Dredd's Wagon of Wonders
The Fantastic Freshman

My Buddy, THE KING

a novel by

BILL BRITTAIN

HARPER & ROW, PUBLISHERS, New York
Grand Rapids, Philadelphia, St. Louis, San Francisco,
London, Singapore, Sydney, Tokyo, Toronto

My Buddy, The King
Copyright © 1989 by William Brittain
Typography by Joyce Hopkins
1 2 3 4 5 6 7 8 9 10
First Edition

Library of Congress Cataloging-in-Publication Data
Brittain, Bill.
   My buddy, the King : a novel / by Bill Brittain.
      p.   cm.
   Summary: When King Tokab of Mokobway is saved from choking
on a frankfurter by Tim Quilt, they become fast friends and together
outwit a plot to do in the king.
   ISBN 0-06-020724-8 : $. — ISBN 0-06-020725-6 (lib. bdg.) : $
   [1. Kings, queens, rulers, etc.—Fiction. 2. Spies—Fiction.
3. Humorous stories.] I. Title.
PZ7.B78067My 1989   88-35704
[Fic]—dc19   CIP
                                                               AC

For Lucille—
Welcome to the family!

Contents

The Heimlich Maneuver   3

SIS-BOOM-BAH   19

King Tokab   38

Around Town   56

Second Attempt   70

Good-bye, My Brother   89

A Bang-up Ending   103

One More Surprise   120

My Buddy,
THE KING

· 1 ·

The Heimlich Maneuver

Okay, Mr. Coffin. Since you *insisted* that your office has to have a report on my week as an agent for the U.S. government, here it is. And I hope you choke on it! It'll probably just get stuck in a file somewhere down there in Washington, under "Quilt, Timothy," to gather dust for the next century or so, if I know you guys.

I guess the whole thing began with Dad coming home from the office on Friday and telling us he was being sent on a ten-day business trip to San Francisco, and Mom was going with him. The trip had come up really sudden, and they were to leave first thing next morning.

Naturally, my sister Laura had a fit. Right

away she started moaning about how she wanted
to go too, and it wouldn't hurt a bit if she missed
one little week of her senior year of high school,
and that she never got to do anything she really
wanted to.

Mom wasn't having any. "It'll be like a second
honeymoon," she told Dad. "Just the two of us."
Then she began planning what she'd wear and
wondering if she could get in any last-minute
shopping before the next morning.

"I am a bit concerned about the kids," said
Dad. "If they get to fighting, we could come
back to a pile of rubble instead of a house."

"Laura's quite old enough to take care of her-
self," Mom told him. "And she can look after
Timmy, too."

Terrific. Now, for ten days, I'd be under
Laura's thumb like a beetle waiting to be
squashed. Anytime she wasn't sitting on the
couch with her idiot boyfriend, Ralph Dean,
she'd be having me do all the dumb work she
didn't want to dirty her hands with. I could just
imagine the way she'd be screeching at me.

"Timothy Quilt, you pick up your room this
minute. . . . Timmy, empty the baskets. . . .
Run the vacuum, Timmy. . . . Mow the lawn,
Timmy. . . ." I was getting sick of it already, and

Mom and Dad hadn't even left yet.

On Saturday morning Mom kissed us both good-bye—she gets a little slushy at times like these—while Dad wrote out a list of who we should call in case of any kind of trouble—from a hangnail to Godzilla coming up out of the ocean and attacking our village. Finally they got into the airport taxi, zoomed out of Wycliff Crescent, and were gone.

Laura was still waving to them when I ducked out the front door. If she was going to put me to work, she had to catch me first. My beat-up old bike was strategically located in the middle of the front walk, and I climbed aboard. As I wobbled past the FOR RENT sign on the front lawn of the house across the street and began picking up speed, I heard Laura yelling after me. "Timmy Quilt, you come back here, you little monster! You have work to do. . . ."

Up . . . up . . . and awayyyy!

Maconville is just like all the rest of the suburban villages that cram Long Island from one end to the other. Five days a week about a billion commuters hop into trains of the Long Island Rail Road and take an hour or so getting to their jobs in New York City. At the end of the day, they all come back again, with the trains so mobbed it must be hard to even breathe. But on Saturday mornings they all head for the village stores to buy grass seed, deck paint, and any other junk they need, to keep their homes and their boats looking better than what their neighbors have. Then they spend the rest of Saturday and all day Sunday working their fingers to the bone and telling themselves they're having a good time. Jeez, people are funny.

I headed downtown, figuring that was where the action was. I stopped in front of Cooley's Drug Store and was looking up and down crowded Main Street when a voice behind me said:

"Hey, Tim. Gimme some skin."

I spun around and gave a high five to Eighty-eight Ruswell. Eighty-eight's my best friend. His real name's Perry, but everybody calls him Eighty-eight. Some say it's because he can play anything from ragtime to Mozart on the eighty-eight keys of a piano, even though he is just fourteen like me. According to others, though, eighty-eight pounds is all he weighs, even though he is nearly six feet tall. I never saw anybody so skinny.

"Hello, Timmy." The short, fat boy behind Eighty-eight stared at me, and his eyes seemed as big as soup bowls. You'd swear, from the expression on his face, that he was terrified the heavens would open up and pour molten lava right on top of his head.

That was Noel (the Coward) Feeney, my other best friend. Noel the Coward's really an okay guy. But with those huge eyes, and lips that are usually pinched up into a little *O*, he always looks like he's scared out of his wits. Eighty-eight and I like having him around though, because he always makes both of us appear as brave as lions.

"Mr. Tim," Eighty-eight said, "what can the three of us do to make this fine day a thrill-a-minute adventure?"

I shrugged. Thrills were hard to come by on a Saturday morning in Maconville.

"We . . . we could go to the Slurp Shoppe and get some ice cream," sputtered Noel the Coward. "If we . . . we had some money. . . ."

"Say no more, just head for the store," chanted Eighty-eight. "It just so happens I provided a little music for the women's club at our church last evening. They paid me ten bucks, and what's money for if you don't spend it? My treat, gentlemen."

If Eighty-eight was ready to buy, I was ready to eat. We lit out for the Slurp Shoppe.

Inside, it was nice and cool, with big fans spinning slowly up near the ceiling. Mr. Kaprides welcomed us as his first customers of the day. It wouldn't get crowded until nearer noon, when all those shoppers would come in for drinks, ice cream, and maybe a hot dog or a hamburger.

We took our favorite booth, way in the back, and Eighty-eight ordered chocolate ice cream all around.

I had my first spoonful halfway to my mouth when all at once the door of the Slurp Shoppe banged open, and two men came in. They were wearing *suits*, for pete's sake, and starched white shirts and neckties. Nobody in Maconville dresses like that on Saturday. The nearest thing to formal wear is usually a sweatshirt with *Maconville Yacht Club* on it.

While Eighty-eight and Noel the Coward and I peered at them over the high back of the booth, the two men looked around like they were casing the place for a robbery. Then they motioned with their hands for whoever was outside to come in.

The next guy who appeared in the doorway made my jaw drop about a foot and my eyebrows shoot up to the part in my hair. He must have been nearly eight feet tall, with shoulders so wide he had to turn sideways and duck at the same time just to get through the opening. His slits of eyes had a mean glitter in them, and his whole face looked like it had been chiseled out of rock. A white scar ran along one cheek, from his ear almost to a corner of his mouth.

The suit he was wearing appeared to be a couple of sizes too small, and his muscles bulged like big lumps of coal under his clothes. On his head he wore a little orange felt hat shaped like a water glass turned upside down, with a tassel that hung over one ear.

The next one to come in was of normal size. In fact he was a bit shorter than normal, and kind of fat. He had a wide red ribbon running from his left shoulder across his chest to his right hip.

These two took places on either side of the door and bowed low from the waist. At that, the kid entered. Okay, he wasn't a kid, except compared to the others. He was about my age, and he was wearing a really sharp gray suit. Even though he didn't have a fancy hat or any ribbons, I could see from the way he held his head high and looked around like he owned the place that he was the one in charge. When he went to a table, the Monster hotfooted it right behind him and pulled out his chair. Then everybody—in-

cluding the two men who'd first entered—
bowed again as the kid sat down.

It was pretty clear nobody was aware of the
three of us in the back booth. While the two
who'd come in first stationed themselves at the
front door of the Slurp Shoppe, the little fat man
gave his order to Mr. Kaprides, who slammed a
hot dog and about three dozen hamburgers on
the grill.

When everything was cooked, Mr. Kaprides
served the hot dog to the boy and put one hamburger in front of the short, fat man. The Monster got everything else and began tossing those
burgers into his mouth like they were popcorn.

Just about then, from outside the store came a
screech of car brakes, followed by the sound of
metal being crunched. Just another fender-
bender auto accident. But the way all those guys
acted, you'd have thought we were being at-
tacked by creatures from Mars. The first two
men sprang to the window and stuck their hands
inside their jackets. The Monster got up, a half-
eaten burger still in his mouth, and stood facing
the door with his arms spread wide. The little fat
man cowered behind the monster and peered
outside.

While they were getting all excited, the boy

remained at the table, tucking away his food.

It was Noel the Coward who first spotted the trouble.

"The boy's choking," he whispered.

He was right. All the men were staring out the window at the accident. Meanwhile the boy, unnoticed by anybody, started clutching at his throat and wriggling in his chair and opening his mouth like he wanted to shout. But he couldn't make a sound. His eyes just got wider and wider, while his face seemed to puff up like air was being pumped into it.

He was going to die right there if somebody didn't do something real quick. I thought of shouting. But I figured if I did, everybody'd pay attention to me instead of the boy needing the help. If anybody was going to *do* anything, it'd have to be me.

In health class in school, we'd learned this thing called the Heimlich maneuver, which you're supposed to do when somebody is choking. But Jeez! I never thought I'd actually have to *use* it.

Outside, the two drivers were screaming words at one another that, if I'd used 'em at home, I'd have had my mouth washed out with soap. They got louder and louder. At the window, the Monster, Fats, and the other two seemed real interested in what was going on out there. Behind them, the boy was quietly going to die unless I got busy real quick!

I pushed my way past Noel the Coward and out of the booth. Scurrying up to the choking boy, I stuck my left hand in his armpit and lifted, pulling him to his feet. At the same time I banged him hard on the back with my right fist.

Then I got around behind him, wrapping my arms about his body and sticking my right fist in the center of his chest, just below his ribs. I grabbed the fist with my other hand. Finally I yanked backward and upward, as hard as I could, driving my balled hands against him.

Nothing. He was still choking. I did it again. Still nothing. Again. . . . Again. . . .

There was a sound like air whizzing out of a tire. At the same time a chunk of hot dog flew across the shop, splatted against a candy case, and fell to the floor.

My arms were still wrapped around the boy, who was greedily breathing in and out as if he'd never get enough air. "Are you all right now?" I asked.

He nodded. But before he could say anything, one of the men behind me at the window must have noticed what was going on, because suddenly there was a voice screaming in my ear.

"One move and you're dead meat, wise guy! Now get those hands up . . . high!"

I looked over my left shoulder and nearly fainted right there on the spot. The man had yanked out a pistol that only needed wheels to be called a cannon. He was pointing it right at me!

To my right, his partner also had me covered. Worst of all, the Monster was standing over me with his arms outstretched. He looked like he was getting ready to wring me like a washcloth.

Where were my friends Eighty-eight and Noel the Coward through all this? The only glimpse I had of them was four eyeballs, peering around the edge of the booth in the rear.

"Put . . . away . . . the . . . guns . . . please," said the boy in a halting voice. Then he murmured something to the Monster in a language I didn't understand. The Monster lowered his arms, though he continued to scowl at me. The guns didn't move an inch.

"I . . . I was choking, you see," the boy went on. "This fellow saved my life. See, there." He pointed to the hunk of hot dog lying on the tiled floor.

Slowly the guns went back into their shoulder holsters. At the same time, Fats and the Monster began chattering to one another in that strange language.

"Are you here all alone, kid?" Big Gun asked me suspiciously.

"No sir. My friends are in the booth back there." With that, Eighty-eight and Noel the Coward came slinking out into the open.

"Jeez, Molloy," said Big Gun to his partner. "You're supposed to check whenever we go in anywhere. These three could have been—well—anybody."

His partner just stared shamefacedly at the floor.

Before we could leave the Slurp Shoppe, Big Gun wanted to know our names, our addresses, and just about everything else except the size of our socks. But finally we were allowed back on Main Street, leaving three dishes of ice cream inside to melt uneaten.

"Beats all," said Eighty-eight. "What a lot of gall. I mean, those guys could have killed you, Tim. And all you were doing was helping out."

"You were real brave, Timmy," said Noel the Coward. "Wait till all the guys hear . . ."

"What are we going to tell 'em that wouldn't sound like we were lying through our teeth?" I said. "If you ask me, that whole bunch of guys came from some insane asylum. And I sure wouldn't want that big one getting mad at me for shooting off my mouth."

"I'm not a fool, I'll stay real cool," said Eighty-eight. "Not a word out of me."

Noel the Coward nodded in agreement.

We strolled down past the hardware store. The blue Rushwind ten-speed racing bike was still in the window. Graphite frame, aluminum wheels, a derailleur that slid through its gears like a hot knife through butter, a weight that was measured in ounces instead of pounds . . . and a price tag of nearly five hundred dollars.

"I would cheerfully give up ice cream for the rest of my life to own that bike," I told Noel the Coward. "I would do the homework of everybody in the class through all four years of high school. I would say good-bye to TV forever. I would . . ."

"It's still pretty expensive, Timmy," said Noel the Coward.

"You sound like my father," I replied. "He says anything over forty bucks for a bike is robbery.

Maybe he's right. But haven't you ever wanted something so much you ached, even though you knew it was impossible to get it? Maybe someday, when I'm old, and real rich, I'll buy myself a bike like that. But I can't help it—I want it now!"

I allowed Eighty-eight to tear me away from the window, and we walked off down the street.

What with checking on all the stores and meeting and talking with all the other guys who were cruising around downtown that day, I didn't get back home until nearly two o'clock. Laura was waiting for me with a broom in one hand and a dustcloth in the other. I could almost see sparks shooting out of her eyes—and ears.

"You worm, Timmy!" she shrieked. "What do you mean, leaving me with all the work around here? Where have you been?"

"Oh, here and there," I said. The last thing I wanted to do was tell Laura about what had happened in the Slurp Shoppe. I just smiled.

"Don't you smirk at me, Timothy Quilt!"

I wanted to tell Laura she didn't need to scream, because I wasn't in Japan or someplace, I was standing right in front of her. But I guessed it was better to let her get it out of her system.

"I certainly have no intention of doing all of what you . . . you 'men' . . . call women's work," Laura went on, with a toss of her head. "So you can just wash up the breakfast dishes and vacuum the rug and dust the living room and . . ."

"Jeez, Laura. Didn't you do anything while I was away?"

Wrong comment. Laura threw the dustcloth at me and then stuck her face about an inch from mine. "Get busy, you tree toad!" she bellowed. "And the first thing you can do is take care of that!"

She pointed to a big box sitting in the corner of the living room. "What is it?" I asked.

"I have no idea, swamp scum. It was delivered here just five minutes ago. And it has your name on it."

I looked curiously at the box. The tag in the center of one side had my name and address, all right. Then I read the print stenciled below the tag, and suddenly I knew what that guy at Sutter's Mill out in California felt like when he struck gold.

RUSHWIND CYCLING COMPANY, INC.
Professional Racing Model A-1 (blue)

Way down at the bottom of the box was the price tag—$498.36. Stamped across it in red ink were three little words that made "I love you" sound about as exciting as "Empty the garbage":

PAID IN FULL

·2·

SIS-BOOM-BAH

I had the brand-new bike I'd been longing for, and the sun was shining, and the whole glorious afternoon stretched out ahead of me. All I wanted to do was put the parts together and go for my first ride.

But do you think Laura would let me go? Anybody who'd answer "yes" to that one doesn't know big sisters very well. "Straighten up your room, worm breath," she began harping at me. "We'll talk about this bike business later. But first, I've got a lot of work for you to do."

She did, too. By the time I was finished, it was nearly suppertime. Then Laura had to inspect everything. "There's dirt in the corners, punk," she'd whine. Or, "You left dust balls under your bed." Yakkety-yak! Someday that sister of mine is going to make a great Marine drill sergeant.

Right in the middle of everything, the phone rang. I made a lunge for it, but Laura got there first. And all of a sudden, the Wicked Witch of the West turned into Miss Charm.

"Why yes, Mrs. Levering," she cooed into the receiver. "Mommy and Daddy have gone away for a few days. An emergency at the store in San Francisco. And Daddy was the only one his company trusted to straighten it out. That's right, Timmy and I are keeping house by ourselves until they get back."

A short pause, while Laura allowed our next-door neighbor to get a few words in. Then: "Thank you for the offer, but we're doing fine by ourselves." A little giggle. "Yes, he can be a problem sometimes. But I guess that's how little brothers are."

She hung up the phone, and quick as a wink, Miss Charm was gone. "Stop standing there with your mouth hanging open!" she screeched at me. "Get back to work!

It wasn't until after supper—with me doing the dishes—that I was allowed to go down in the cellar and start assembling my new bike. Even then, Laura stuck to me like glue.

"Timmy Quilt, I demand to know where you got that bike. Did you take the money out of your savings account? That's supposed to be for your college education. If Daddy finds out . . ."

"Hold on, moss brain. I didn't take any money out of . . ."

"Oh, no! So it's stolen property! What will my friends say when they find out my brother's a thief? I'll be shamed forever!"

"Don't be a total idiot. The box was delivered here. And it has my name on it."

"Yes, but who sent it?"

"How should I know? Maybe I won a lottery or something. But now it's mine, all right. And I'm keeping it."

Laura jabbered on. Shutting that girl up is like trying to dam the Mississippi with a handful of sand. Then, along about eight o'clock, I got lucky.

The doorbell upstairs rang. That had to be Laura's boyfriend, Ralph Dean. Ralph's a real jerk. He always tries to talk like those fancy guys who go to exclusive schools in New England. You know, like he has a cork up his nose. He'd be wearing a sport jacket with a matching tie and loafers with a shine like mirrors.

No, I can't see through walls. But that's the kind of dumb clothes Ralph *always* wears.

This Saturday night, for the first time ever, I was glad to have him put in an appearance. Anything to get my sister off my back.

Laura and Ralph went out, and I was left in peace with my new bicycle. First thing, I grabbed the phone to call Eighty-eight and Noel the Coward and do a little discreet bragging.

Just my luck. No answer at either number. I consoled myself by imagining the looks on their faces when I saw them in school and announced my good news.

I could hardly wait until morning, when I could ride my Rushwind Professional Racing Bicycle all over town.

On Sunday, when Laura and I got home from church, we saw we were getting new neighbors. And from the looks of things, they were going to be really *strange* new neighbors.

Wycliff Crescent is a little dead-end street. Laura keeps telling me I shouldn't say "dead-end," because "cul-de-sac" sounds more elegant. To me it just sounds dumb.

Anyway, there are only two houses besides ours on Wycliff Crescent. The Leverings, an old retired couple who keep pretty much to themselves, live next to us. Then there's the big place across the street that has a front porch around three sides of it and enough land to hold army maneuvers. It'd had a FOR RENT sign on it for the past couple of months.

As we walked home from church—I'd wanted to ride my new bike, but Laura about had a fit—we saw the sign was gone and a moving van was backed up in the driveway. The porch was full of furniture, and a couple of guys in coveralls were shoehorning a sofa through the door. But that wasn't the odd part.

Men wearing white shirts, and ties, were crawling all over the property. And I mean crawling, with most of 'em down on their hands and knees in the dirt. They were inspecting the foundation and peering in through the windows and taking measurements from all the trees and bushes, and there was even one guy in a suit up on the pole in front, putting in a couple of new phone lines.

Riding my new bike could wait.

Laura and I brought some potato chips and soda into our living room and sat staring out our big front window like we were watching television. But this was better than TV. This was real.

"Timmy." Laura suddenly pointed toward one of the men who seemed to be checking the dirt by the porch. "Something dropped out of his jacket. It looks like . . . it *is*! That man's carrying a gun!"

Inside my head a big alarm bell started ringing. I remembered looking down the muzzle of a gun in the Slurp Shoppe, just yesterday. It had been like staring into a cave. Now, here were some of the same kind of men, right across the street. What was going on?

Well, I wasn't going over there to ask, that was for sure.

The moving van left. The men in suits stayed. A little later another truck rolled up and some workmen got out.

"Hey look," I said. "They're putting up a fence."

"They certainly are," said Laura. "Chain link, six feet high, and . . . and with barbed wire at the top. What are they planning on doing over there—raising gorillas?"

By dusk, everything was finished. The house across the street from us now looked like a prison, with the single big gate in the fence locked shut in three places. In the gloom I could see a few of those guys in suits moving about the property like they expected an attack at any moment.

Lying in bed that night, I tried to make myself believe everything I'd seen was just a dream. But when I got up for school, the fence was still there. So were the guys with the suits . . . and the guns.

Don't even try and ask me what went on in math and English, my first two classes on Monday. All I could think of was what had happened to me in the Slurp Shoppe . . . getting a new Rushwind bicycle out of the blue . . . and the house across the street that now looked like San Quentin, complete with guards. When I saw Eighty-eight and Noel the Coward in the halls and told them everything that'd happened since I had left them on Saturday morning, they about flipped.

"Sounds to me like you got some big-time gangsters moving in on you, Tim," said Eighty-eight. "Have you been payin' off your gambling debts regular? Them dudes don't like it when you hold out on 'em."

"Maybe it's beings from another planet," suggested Noel the Coward. "They're getting ready to put you in a flying saucer and . . . ZOOM!"

I didn't think they were being funny. But then, maybe they weren't trying to be funny.

A little after ten thirty, I was in social studies class, and Mr. Vedder was trying, without much success, to get us interested in the travels of Marco Polo when the intercom phone buzzed. Mr. Vedder answered, looked straight at me, and said, "Sure, he's here."

He hung up and pointed a long finger. "Tim Quilt, you're wanted in the principal's office."

Great. What had I done now? I ticked down through my list of school sins for the past week. Okay, I'd copied Noel the Coward's French homework. But I hadn't even handed it in yet. In our school golf tournament last week, I'd given myself a two-foot putt I should have tapped in. Our team lost anyway. My locker was messy, but who knew as long as I kept the door closed?

I couldn't figure it. Why would the principal want to see *me*?

I got a pass from Mr. Vedder and schlumphed down to the main office. The secretary pointed to the door with VICTOR BESSINGER, PH.D.—

PRINCIPAL lettered on it. "You can go right in, Timothy," she said.

I went right in. There wasn't a light on in the place, and the curtains had been pulled across the windows. It was as gloomy as Count Dracula's castle.

I could just dimly see the outline of the man seated at the principal's desk. He was wide and heavy, and he had his arms out pressing down on the desk like he was trying to shove it through the floor. From what little I could see, he didn't look like anybody I knew. He sure wasn't Dr. Bessinger. Dr. Bessinger is small and skinny.

"Are you Quilt?" rumbled the man.

"Yes, s-sir."

"Timothy Quilt, of 17 Wycliff Crescent? Family made up of your parents; one sister, Laura; and you—is that right?"

"Yes. But how did you know . . ."

There was a soft click, and the desk light went on. The man looked tough and mean, with a nose that'd been broken at least three times, clay-gob ears that seemed glued to his head, and a chin like the blade of a bulldozer. He wore a blue pinstripe suit, and since the jacket was unbuttoned, I could see the glint of a pistol parked in his left armpit.

I felt the hairs on the back of my neck begin to prickle. Scared? I was terrified!

"Siddown, Quilt," said the man, pointing to a chair at one end of the desk. "I'm Coffin."

"If you're coughin', you ought to see a doctor," I said. "A cold is nothing to be sneezed at." Okay, it wasn't the best joke in the world. Still, the guy could have at least chuckled.

No way. He sat there staring at me like I was an insect on the end of a pin.

"Your principal, Dr. Bessinger, was kind enough to lend me his office so we could talk," he went on in a voice that rumbled like distant thunder. "My *name's* Coffin—Jacob Coffin. I'm from SIS-BOOM-BAH."

"SIS-BOOM-BAH, sir?" It was all I could do to hold back a nervous giggle. The guy sounded like he was leading a cheer for the football team.

"That's right, Quilt. Did you ever hear of it?"

"No, sir."

"Good. We don't like having our name too well known. But here. This'll explain things."

He shoved a hand as big as a phone book toward me. Between two lumpy fingers was what looked like a business card. I took it.

At the top was our country's seal—an eagle clutching arrows and an olive branch—and the words *U.S. Government.* Below that, I read:

Security Intelligence Service – SIS
Bureau Of Operational Methods – BOOM
Beginning-Agent Headquarters – BAH

At the very bottom was his name: *Jacob Coffin— Director.*

Intelligence. . . . Agent. . . . The words whirled through my mind as I stared at Coffin, dumfounded. "You're a spy!" I yipped finally.

"Quiet, Quilt!" snapped Coffin, looking about furtively. "I don't want the whole world to know what we're talking about here."

"But I'm not an enemy agent. Why are you investigating me?"

"We're not investigating you," said Coffin with a little chuckle. "In fact, Uncle Sam wants you to work for him for a few days."

"Me? A spy?"

"You make it sound like we were going to send you to some foreign country with a bomb in your pocket," said Coffin. "It's not that way at all. Okay, SIS-BOOM-BAH is a secret organization. But our job is to look after foreign visitors to this country—important visitors. We find out about their customs and what's necessary to keep 'em happy while they're here. We also protect 'em if there's a threat against their lives."

"Secret organization . . ." I murmured. "Threats. . . . It sure sounds like spying. But what do you want with me?"

Coffin leaned back in his chair. "Did you ever hear of a country called Mokobway, Quilt?"

"No, sir."

"I'm not surprised. It's a little place—only about a hundred square miles."

"But where . . . where's it located?"

Coffin brushed the question aside with a wave of his hand. "Not important," he snapped. "All you need to know is that it's one of the third-world nations, and up until twenty-five years ago it was mostly wilderness, with the people living in huts and hunting their dinner with rocks and arrows. Then, back in the sixties, a couple of geologists found that Mokobway is sitting on one of the biggest pools of oil in the entire world."

"Oil?" I said. "That's pretty important now-adays."

"It sure is," Coffin agreed. "So every industrial nation in the world—including ours—began try-ing to gain influence in Mokobway. But it's a strange nation. It's pretty well cut off from the rest of the world, and its rulers seem to like it that way. Oh, in some ways it's becoming more modernized. The capitol building is made of brick and mortar, and it even has electricity. There're maybe five miles of paved roads.

"But they have almost no knowledge of how people in other countries live, and a lot of their customs are still very primitive. The national bird is the buzzard. All their official sports are played while hopping on one leg, and broiled lizard is considered a great delicacy, to be served only on the most formal occasions. The king controls nearly all the wealth, and he has absolute power. One word from him, and a man can get his head chopped off just for spitting on a trail through the forest."

"That king doesn't sound like somebody I'd like to meet up with," I said.

At that, Coffin slammed his hands down onto the desk and leaned forward until his nose almost touched mine. "That's the reason I chased the principal out of his office so you and I could have this talk, Quilt," he said in a low voice. "You've already met Tokab—the king of Mokobway. On Saturday morning, you saved his life in the Slurp Shoppe."

At that, my mind began whirling like a record turntable. "Those . . . those guys who were looking the place over . . ."

"My men," said Coffin.

"That great, huge . . ."

"The royal bodyguard."

"The little fat . . ."

"Elo dar Quaman, the prime minister."

"The boy with the hot dog stuck . . ."

"King Tokab himself. He's just about your age. And since you saved him from choking to death, he feels he owes you a great debt. Right now he thinks more highly of you than of anybody else in the world."

"Oh." Then something else occurred to me. "The bicycle," I gasped. "Did he . . . ?"

Coffin nodded. "Tokab had one of my men follow you with instructions to buy you anything you admired. For what it's worth, Quilt, the king would have bought you the whole hardware store—or even the city hall—if you thought you wanted it."

"But what's the king—King Tokab—doing in Maconville?" I asked. "Why isn't he back in Mokobway, sitting on his throne and . . . and doing whatever kings do?"

"Tokab's in the U.S. to give a speech at the

United Nations," answered Coffin. "Frankly, SIS-BOOM-BAH would have preferred to keep him in a hotel in New York, under tight security. But after Tokab arrived, he decided he wanted to visit those 'suburbs' he'd heard about and maybe get some ideas for public housing back in Mokobway. The State Department chose Maconville as being fairly typical. And now, because of you, the king wants to remain right here until after his U.N. speech."

"Then . . . then he's the one who rented . . ."

"That's right. He'll be living just across the street from you. We had less than twenty-four hours to turn the place into a maximum security compound. Quite a job, but when our government wants something done fast, it has a way of getting done."

"But I still don't understand where I fit into all this."

"Tokab wants you—the one who saved his life—as a companion while he's in the U.S. And because of all that oil, whatever Tokab wants, Tokab gets."

"Great," I moaned. "And the first time I spit on the sidewalk, I discover my head's no longer attached to my shoulders—is that it?"

"You still don't get it. According to Mokobway

tradition, having saved the king's life, you're like a brother to him. Nobody else—except maybe the president—can approach the king without all kinds of bowing and scraping and saluting. But you could go up and spit in his *eye*, and he wouldn't say 'boo.' That's what makes you so valuable. For your country's sake, Timothy Quilt, you've got to be King Tokab's companion for the next week or so. Make friends with him. Get him to like you enough so we can get the rights to all that oil."

"What about school?" I asked. "How can I be with the king if I'm in . . ."

"You'll be excused from school."

"But I've got tests coming up in . . ."

Coffin waved this objection aside. "You'll get A$^+$ on every test, even if you don't take it. I'll see to that."

All *right*! Maybe this spy business wouldn't be so bad after all.

"Will I get to carry a gun? And maybe a radio in the heel of my shoe, and . . ."

"No, Quilt. You'll be a WOWIE agent."

"A what?"

"WOWIE—'Without Weapons or Intelligence Equipment.' We're not going to have a fourteen-year-old kid shooting up the town or playing with a radio and jamming every TV station on Long Island."

"Mr. Coffin?"

"Yeah, Quilt?"

"If I'm gonna do this, I don't ever want you calling me a kid again. Is that understood?" I suddenly knew SIS-BOOM-BAH needed me.

Coffin's eyes flashed angrily as he stared at me. Then the eyes dropped. "Okay, Quilt."

This was power. I *loved* it!

"One more thing," Coffin went on. "We don't expect any trouble with Tokab's visit. But if something does come up, you're to contact Agent Arlo Dexter. He's our chief GOOSE."

"*Goose?* I'm going to be talking with a *bird*?"

" 'Government Operative, On Site— Equipped,' " said Coffin. "Dexter's head of the team actually guarding Tokab. In addition to being armed, Dexter has a two-way radio and can be in contact with me, the FBI, and even the Army, Navy, and Marines within seconds. Of course, you're never to get in touch with me unless something comes up that Dexter can't handle."

"If you're not there, how do I find you?" I asked.

"Pick up a phone and dial the letters SIS-

BOOM-BAH. But only in an emergency. Your job, Agent Quilt, is just to make the king like you enough to release that oil to our country. So forget about the cloak-and-dagger routine. Got that?"

"Yes, sir."

"Let's try and keep this whole thing as secret as we can. No telling what you're doing to every Tom, Dick, and Harry. Understood?"

"Uh-huh. Can I tell my sister?"

"I guess so. She's bound to find out anyway."

"And my friends, Eighty-eight Ruswell and Noel Feeney?"

"Only if it's absolutely necessary."

"And the guys on the golf team and the student council and . . ."

"Quilt!" Coffin's face got bright red. "Stop it! I'm your boss now."

"Yes, boss," I said. "Just one more thing."

"What's that?"

"How much does the job pay?"

"You'll be working for your country, Quilt. Isn't that enough?"

"You work for your country, boss. But you get paid, don't you?"

Coffin nodded. "How about a hundred bucks?"

"How about a thousand?"

"Quilt, you are a greedy kid . . . I mean, agent. But I think I can get you the thousand dollars out of our special fund."

I stood up and threw Coffin a salute that would have made a drill sergeant proud. "Then Agent Timothy Quilt stands ready to do his patriotic duty . . . sir!"

·3·

King Tokab

It was a little after noon when Coffin signed me out of school and drove me back to Wycliff Crescent. He pulled up by the gate of the chain-link fence and signaled to one of the men in business suits who were standing in the front yard and glancing around like they expected a dragon or something to pop out of the bushes.

"This is Agent Dexter . . . our chief GOOSE, remember?" said Mr. Coffin as the man unlocked the gate. We walked into the yard, and Dexter shook hands with me. He looked to be about thirty years old, with freckles and sandy hair that wouldn't stay combed.

"Call me Arlo, Tim," said Dexter with a friendly smile. "I'm your contact here, and if you need anything—anything at all—I can arrange to get it. Whether it's a moving van or a set of bagpipes you need to keep the king happy, I can have it in less than an hour."

"How about a gun?" I asked. I still had visions of being like James Bond.

Coffin's face started getting red, but Arlo kept his cool. I liked that. "No gun for you," Arlo said with a chuckle. "This assignment's a piece of cake. Everything calm and peaceful."

As Coffin returned to the car, Arlo relocked the gate and led me around to the backyard. King Tokab and his prime minister, the little fat Elo dar Quaman, were sitting on the grass, wearing sport shirts that shrieked with color. Clipped to the prime minister's belt was a little plastic box with a button on it. It looked something like the beeper Dad sometimes wears when he's away from the office.

Just behind King Tokab stood the gigantic bodyguard, still wearing his lumpy suit, and with an expression on his face like a charging rhinoceros.

Tokab spotted us and sprang to his feet. Arlo made the introductions. "His Supreme and Royal Majesty, King Tokab of Mokobway . . . Prime Minister Elo dar Quaman . . . and this big fella is Arbata Oman Kaba, but we all call him Fez on account of that hat he always wears. May I present—"

But before Arlo could give my name, King Tokab wrapped his arms about me in a huge hug. "Timothy Quilt," he said with a smile. "My savior. May I call you Tim?"

"Call . . . call me anything you like, your majesty," I sputtered. It wasn't easy, doing the king bit with a boy just about my own age. "I'm very honored to—"

" 'Your majesty,' indeed!" scoffed King Tokab. "You saved my life, Tim, and so we are like brothers, you and I. To you, I am just Tokab."

Then he leaned forward, putting his mouth very close to my ear. "Sometimes it grows tiresome, being a king," he whispered so that only I could hear. "I would love just to be a boy for a while, and not always be dealing with pompous and bootlicking grown-ups. I hope you and I will become—as you say—'good buddies.' Are you agreeable to that?"

"Sure," I breathed with a little nod of my head. "I'd like that, too, Tokab."

"Good, good." He drew his lips away from my ear and spoke louder. "Then shake hands with Elo dar Quaman. I alone call him Elo. But I extend to you the same privilege."

"Your majesty!" the prime minister protested. "I hardly think it dignified for a complete stranger to call me—"

"This 'stranger' saved my life, Elo," said Tokab. "He is worthy of such informality. Elo it shall be, Tim."

As I shook Elo's pudgy hand, Tokab turned to me and winked, like he'd gotten a big kick out of putting the prime minister in his place. "And this is my bodyguard, Fez. From this moment, he will protect you as diligently as he does me. Do you understand, Fez?"

Fez bowed to Tokab, glared at me like he wanted to tear me limb from limb, and grasped my hand in one extended paw. I was really relieved when I got my hand back with no parts missing or damaged.

"You will all leave us now," Tokab ordered, glancing around at Elo, Fez, and a couple of Arlo's guards who had wandered by.

"But your majesty," said Elo. "There is much to be made ready before—"

"Leave us, wretched one," snapped Tokab. "Else I shall have Fez tie each of your fingers into intricate knots."

Fez was just the guy who could do it, too. Oh,

it did my heart good to hear Tokab ordering around the pompous little man that way. Elo waddled into the house, the guards went back to their places, and Fez plodded to the far side of the yard.

Tokab sat down on the grass and motioned me to a place beside him. "You must tell me all about life here in the United States, Tim," he said. "In Mokobway, you see, I learned only what my advisors wished me to know of your country. And they consider me but a boy, even though I am also their king."

"Let me see," I replied, trying to remember everything I'd been told in school about our government. "Well, our leader is called the president, and he lives in Washington, our capital. Then there's the Senate and the House of Representatives. Their job is to make the laws and—"

"Oh, bother the political structure!" Tokab said impatiently. "I learned all about that from Elo's unending lectures. I want to know the important things."

"Like what?" I asked.

"What do you do for fun, Tim?"

"Oh. Well, I like playing golf."

"Golf? What is that?"

I gave Tokab a quick explanation. It wasn't

easy. I thought everybody in the world knew how to play golf.

"So you strike a ball with clubs," said Tokab when I'd finished, "and try to roll it into a hole in the ground. There hardly seems to be much point in such a sport."

"Oh yeah? What kind of sports do you have in Mokobway?"

"Our most popular one is called *nipaki.* One has to see how far he can travel from a given spot while hopping on one leg and balancing a staff on the palm of the opposite hand, before one either loses his balance or the staff topples. I've become quite good at it."

I tried to imagine playing a game like *nipaki.* "That's really dumb," I said finally.

"Dumb? You call dumb the national game of Mokobway? Striking a ball until it falls into a hole, which is your . . . your 'golf'—*that* is really dumb."

"It is not."

"Is so."

"No."

"Yes."

Then we both stared at the ground in silence. Great! I'd known the king about five minutes, and here I was, arguing with him. Good-bye, oil. Besides, I really *liked* Tokab. I didn't want to . . .

That's when I felt his hand, gripping my arm. "Tim?"

"Yeah, Tokab?"

"Let us be friends again."

"Yeah!" I agreed. "I . . . I guess if I was a king like you, our countries might have been at war by now."

"Tell me more about the golf."

"Well, I'm on the golf team at school, and—"

"School?" Tokab was staring at me in amazement. "You go to school? Then your family must be of the ruling class."

"Heck, no. Everybody goes to school. Sometimes it's a big pain, but they make us go anyway."

"Everybody goes?" Tokab's mouth hung open. "Girls too?"

"Sure. In a lot of my classes, they're smarter than the boys."

"Girls going to school," he said with a shake of his head. "Astounding. What's the world coming to?"

Then he started blushing, and he lowered his head. "Are they pretty, Tim? The girls, I mean."

"Oh . . . uh . . . well . . . They're all right—most

of 'em. Ellen Harrison in my math class is really a . . . I mean, she's kind of cute."

"I will be married within the next twelve months," said Tokab, none too happily. "I'm told my bride-to-be is a ravishing beauty."

"Told?" I said, astonished. "You mean you haven't seen her?"

The king shook his head. "I won't, until the wedding day. But all has been arranged."

"But how can you . . . I mean, aren't you kind of young to . . ."

"I am a king," said Tokab. "It is the custom. What can I do?"

We talked for a long time after that, about pets (Tokab had a snake in his palace that he sometimes wore like a necklace) and games (he was a whiz at chess but had never heard of Monopoly)—and anything else we could think of. Toward the end, I found it hard to think of Tokab as being the ruler of anywhere. He was just my buddy—my buddy, the king.

Then, out of the corner of my eye, I spotted Fez, striding toward us. I pretended to look at my watch and then jumped to my feet.

"Jeez, I've got to go home," I announced. "It's nearly five, and my sister doesn't know where I am. She'll be having a fit."

"Then I bid you good-bye for now," said Tokab. "You will, of course, be returning for dinner. We'll be eating promptly at eight."

"Aw, Tokab, I don't think . . ." I began. Then, over the king's shoulder, I spotted Fez, looking stern and clenching his fists. "Sure, Tokab. Whatever you say."

How's that for a classy exit line?

As I'd expected, Laura was fuming again when I got home. For about half an hour I tried to tell her what had happened that day, from Jacob Coffin and SIS-BOOM-BAH to meeting Elo and Fez, and talking all afternoon with Tokab—a real king.

Finally I practically dragged her out of the house and across the street to the high fence. Arlo came over to the inside of the wire, and I had him show Laura his identification. Then I went through my story all over again.

"Your brother's telling the truth, Miss Quilt," said Arlo. "But we'd appreciate it if you'd keep a lid on what you've heard and not spread it all over town. We'd like to keep King Tokab's visit here kind of low-key."

You can't imagine how wonderful it was, watching my dumb sister's jaw drop halfway down to her socks.

"But dinner?" she sputtered. "With a king? I mean, if Timmy's going to come, couldn't I . . . that is . . ."

"If you'd like to come along, I'm sure it could be arranged," said Arlo. "Though I suspect you'll find the arrangements somewhat different from what you're used to."

Then Laura threw the big monkey wrench into the gears. "I have this friend—a boy I know," she said, smiling sweetly. "I really don't want to impose, but if he could escort me . . ."

"Aw, come on, Laura!" I sputtered. "Tokab and I are just getting to be friends. I don't want Ralph the Jerk there, lousing things up and . . ."

Arlo kind of chuckled. "I'm sure King Tokab wouldn't mind," he said. "But it's your decision, Tim."

Laura put her hands on her hips and stood there glaring at me.

What could I say? King Tokab would be leaving in a few days. But Laura would be my sister for the rest of our lives.

"Oh . . . I guess so," I grumbled.

Back in our house, Laura called Ralph and *commanded* him to call for her at seven o'clock.

Then she started planning what she'd wear.

By seven thirty we were ready. I had on my best suit, Laura wore the dress she'd been saving for the Senior Prom, and Ralph was in his usual uniform—prep school tie, and the jacket with the patches at the elbows. We went across the street, and Arlo opened the gate.

Inside the house, I introduced Laura and Ralph to Tokab, Elo, and Fez. It did my heart good to see Fez sneer at Ralph. The bodyguard didn't just hate *me.* He hated *everybody.*

"What a marvelous table setting!" exclaimed Laura, spotting the dining room and whirling into it with her skirt flaring around her. She rested her hand on the chair at the head of the table.

"Perhaps, as the only lady present, I should sit here, and have all you fine gentlemen . . ."

Then her voice trailed off as everybody looked at her like she'd just suggested setting fire to the house.

"Excuse me, Miss Quilt," said Elo, scuttling up to her and taking her arm. "But that is his majesty's chair. For you to take it would be an insult punishable by death, were we in Mokobway."

"But I didn't mean to . . ." sputtered Laura. "I mean, I . . ."

She put a hand to her mouth and looked at Fez, terrified. Me? I was loving every minute of it.

"A perfectly natural error, Miss Quilt," said Tokab. "You need not worry about my taking offense. But the seating is all arranged. Tim, as the guest of honor, will sit on my right, with my bodyguard on my left. You may take your place just there—between Fez and Elo."

Laura sat, looked up at the giant next to her, and looked like she wanted to slide right under the table. Across from her, Ralph Dean stared at the tablecloth and, for once, kept his mouth shut.

"May I say how charming it is to have a lady grace this table, Miss Quilt," said Tokab. "In Mokobway, such a thing would be unheard of at a state dinner."

Laura blushed at the compliment, and a little later I caught her glaring at me for being in the place of honor. So I knew she was back to being her old sweet self.

"I have given serious thought to your comments of this afternoon, Tim," Tokab told me. "There is so much to be done in Mokobway. I find fascinating, for example, your country's practice of educating everyone."

"The musings of an American boy are hardly

the stuff on which to build policy in Mokobway, your majesty," said Elo. "If we are to remain in power . . ."

"Power means nothing to me," replied Tokab. "I want only what is best for my people. And I think you, Tim, have much to teach me."

Elo started to reply, but just then servants started coming from the kitchen, carrying large trays.

The dinner was really good. We had roast beef and asparagus and yams. Then came another dish that I'd never seen before. It was a kind of yellow sauce with crunchy things inside that I thought were peanuts. It tasted delicious. I asked Elo about it.

"A great delicacy in Mokobway," he said, "and very nourishing. It is gravied termites."

At that, my stomach started lurching up and down like a bucking horse. I thought I was going to embarrass myself right there at the table. Clamping my teeth together, I slurped some water and finally managed to swallow my mouthful of termites.

Laura made a gasping sound deep in her throat and slapped a hand over her mouth. At the same time, Ralph Dean covered his face with his napkin, got up, and ran toward the front door.

"Tim?" said Tokab. "Miss Quilt? Are you all right?"

"Just . . . just fine, Tokab," I gurgled. "I guess I'm just not used to such rich food."

The life of a secret agent isn't always an easy one.

A little later, Ralph returned, pale and dizzy, supported by two of Arlo Dexter's men. "I . . . I must be coming down with the flu or something," Ralph whispered. "I don't know what came over me."

Much as I loathed Ralph, I had to admit that was a nice recovery.

"What . . . what's it really like, being a king, Tokab?" I asked, a little later, toying with a helping of something that looked like green lard that had thick, squirmy things in it. "I think it'd be real neat, ruling a whole country."

"It is often, as you Americans say, 'a big pain in the neck,' " he told me. "Always, I must wear the royal robes, which are heavy and make me itch. Every moment of every day is planned for me, and I have little or no time to myself. Yet all the important decisions are left to Elo because of my youth. Often, as I watch people fishing in the stream that runs by the palace, I long to join them and be, for a little while, just a boy, rather than a king."

"You . . . you've never been fishing?" I asked, surprised.

Tokab shook his head. "Elo says it is not considered dignified for a king to catch his own food."

"But it's fun!"

"A king has little time for fun, Tim."

Jeez! If that was what being a king was like, I'd rather keep on living in my own house—even with Laura.

It was about ten o'clock when the evening ended. Laura and Ralph said their good-byes and headed back across the street—probably looking for a bottle of mouthwash to get rid of the taste of those termites. As if by magic, everybody—including the servants, Elo, and even Fez—disappeared, leaving Tokab and me alone.

"I . . . I don't think your bodyguard likes me, Tokab," I told him. "Fez kept scowling at me from behind your chair all evening. It was scary."

"Fez's job is to glare and intimidate," said Tokab. "Pay no attention. You are safer under his watchful eye than with all those agents your government saw fit to station here."

"Well . . . okay, if you say so."

"Tomorrow we will talk more of the golf and of the school and of your delightful life in this grand nation. I have much to learn, and you will be my teacher. Sleep well, Timothy Quilt. And may nothing ever mar the friendship between us."

"That goes double for me, Tokab," I replied. Okay, it wasn't a great speech. But I meant every word of it.

I walked outside. Through the window of our house across the street I could see Laura and Ralph. They were yelling at one another. Whistling a jaunty tune, I approached the gate in the high fence, open for me and guarded by one of Arlo's agents.

As I walked out of the king's yard, the lights of a car went on down at the end of Wycliff Crescent. I heard a starter whir and then the motor roared, just as the gate slammed behind me. I waited for the car to pass.

It wasn't going to pass! Those two headlights were pointing right at me. I couldn't get away. My back was already against the fence.

I leaped to the side just as the car reached me.

The edge of the front bumper grazed my ankle, and the car struck the fence with a rattle of vibrating wire. Whoever was in there had lost control, I thought, and almost killed me.

Then the car backed away from the fence. "Hey!" I yelled. "Be careful!"

The car turned and again headed right at me. The near miss hadn't been an accident. It was car tag—and I was *it*!

In the road, I ran this way and that, trying to avoid that glittering front bumper. The car followed my every move.

I turned and ran, as fast as I could. But I knew I could never outdistance an automobile. It got closer . . . closer . . .

At the last possible moment, with the bumper actually brushing my knees, I took a flying leap into the slot between Mr. Levering's oak tree and his picket fence. The car swerved after me.

Crash! The car hit the oak tree, the front end crumpled, and suddenly there was steam everywhere. Across the street I heard the clang of the gate opening and footsteps running toward me.

Suddenly somebody's hand pressed against my chest.

"Don't kill me!" I squealed. "Please!"

"Remain calm, Timothy," said a familiar

voice. "It's only me."

Relief flooded over me as, in the dim glow of the streetlight, I saw the sweaty, pudgy face of Elo dar Quaman staring down at me.

"The car . . ." I panted. "Somebody tried to . . ."

"The agents from your government came to your aid at the same time I did," said Elo. "I'm sure they will deal with the driver in whatever manner is proper."

I allowed Elo to help me to my feet. Behind him I could see Arlo Dexter yanking open the car's door. He looked inside and I saw his head shake as if he were puzzled. Pulling the adjustment lever, he slammed the seat back as far as it would go and knelt down to examine the floor. A little flashlight in his hand lit up first the front seats, then the back.

"Have the whole team spread out and search the yards around here," Arlo ordered crisply. "There's nobody inside the car!"

·4·

Around Town

"Look, it was probably just an accident."

The guy being so cool about my nearly getting killed was Jacob Coffin. I'd called him as soon as I'd gotten home. Now he, Arlo Dexter, Laura, and I were sitting in our kitchen, and there were enough government agents outside to guard the Pentagon. It was nearly one o'clock in the morning.

"I tell you, that car was trying to run me down," I protested. "Every time I swerved, it swerved after me."

"What did you find out, Dexter?" Coffin asked Arlo.

"The car was stolen from a driveway in the next block about forty-five minutes before Tim came out," Arlo said. "My men searched all around here after the crash, but they couldn't find a trace of whoever was driving."

"That's strange," said Coffin. "We've got enough men to cover this area like a tent. How could the guy get away?"

Arlo just shrugged. "It was awful dark out there, chief."

"Mr. Coffin," I said in a quavery voice, "when you asked me to work for SIS-BOOM-BAH, you said I'd just be a buddy to King Tokab. You didn't mention anything about my getting killed."

"For what it's worth, I don't think the car was after you," said Coffin.

"Then who . . . ?"

"The king. Look, Tokab's the absolute ruler of Mokobway. But let's face it—he's just a kid, with a lot of ideas for improving his country, but no political savvy at all. He wants to make things better for his people, but all his advice comes from his royal council. And there are men on that council who'd rather see Tokab dead than have him make changes that would force them to give up a lot of their power."

Coffin scratched his head. "The problem is, none of the royal council came to the U.S. with Tokab. Just the king himself, his prime minister, and that bodyguard."

"Yeah, the bodyguard," I told him. "That Fez hates me. I can tell just by the way he looks at me. I'll bet he was the one driving that car!"

Coffin thought about this. "He *has* got keys to open the gate and get out," he said. "Just like Tokab and Elo dar Quaman. On the other hand, Tokab trusts Fez completely. No, I don't think . . ."

"But if you're wrong, Timmy dies, is that it?" asked Laura primly. It was amazing. My sister really cared about me. "You get him out of this ridiculous and dangerous situation, Mr. Coffin—right now!"

"The king would take that as a terrible insult," said Coffin with a shake of his head. "He could get so angry he'd start selling that oil to . . . to places we'd rather not see it go."

"If I die," I said, "I won't care who gets the oil."

"Tim, your government needs you—badly," Coffin told me. "But we owe you protection. Tell you what—no more meetings with the king after dark. And we'll double the guard. That way, nobody'll be able to get near you without our say-so."

I still wasn't sure.

"What'll it take, Tim? A new sports car the day you get your driver's license? Four years of college all paid for? Whatever you want, I can arrange it."

If Mr. Coffin was trying to bribe me, it worked like a charm. I agreed to go on being Tokab's buddy. "And can I carry a gun now?" I asked hopefully.

Both Coffin and Arlo shook their heads. "You'd just shoot yourself in the foot," chuckled Coffin. "But all my regular men will be armed to the teeth, you can be sure of that."

That really didn't make me feel much better. I didn't get to sleep until after three.

I slept until nearly ten o'clock. When I woke up, through my bedroom window I saw a man walking back and forth in the side yard. One of my guards.

On the kitchen table was a note from Laura saying she'd already left for school. At the bottom, the words *BE CAREFUL!* had been underlined about a million times.

After I'd dressed, I opened the front door. Two more guards were waiting to escort me across the street. King Tokab and Fez were standing at the gate.

"Tim, I most humbly apologize for what occurred last evening," said Tokab. "It was, of course, myself who was the intended victim. A sad and frightening error by whoever was driving that car. I have instructed Fez to guard you with special diligence. No one will harm you while he is around."

Great. All I had to do was be alone with Fez for five minutes, and he'd tear me limb from limb. But how could I tell Tokab that?

"Today, we shall visit your school," the king continued. "All arrangements have been made. The cars are waiting for us."

There were three limousines in the driveway, long and shiny and pointed toward the street. We got into the backseat of the middle one, with Tokab seated between Fez and me. As Coffin prepared to close the door, he suddenly leaned inside and stared first at Tokab and then at me.

"School!" he snarled. "We're trying to keep Tokab's visit under wraps, and now he wants to visit a school. No way we can put a lid on things now. It'll be in the papers and everything, and effective security will be almost impossible. Was this your idiotic idea, Quilt?"

Before I could say anything, Tokab spoke up. "It was my wish, Mr. Coffin, for which I take full responsibility. If you have a complaint, make it to me directly. Well?"

Coffin just stared at Tokab, his mouth opening and closing like a dying fish. He made an angry sound deep in his throat and then slammed the car door—hard.

Our little motorcade zoomed through the streets of Maconville and into the school parking lot, where a bunch of uniformed policemen and Dr. Bessinger, the principal, were waiting for us. Tokab, Fez, and I walked to Dr. Bessinger's office surrounded by enough guards to hold off the 7th Army.

"If there is anything you desire, your majesty, to make your tour more enjoyable," said Dr. Bessinger, "you have only to ask." Oh, it did my heart good to see my principal bowing and scraping before the fourteen-year-old Tokab.

"I can think of nothing," the king replied. "How about you, Tim?"

"No, everything's just . . ." Then I had a really great idea. "Yeah. I'd like Eighty-eight—I mean, Perry Ruswell—and Noel Feeney to come along, too."

Mr. Bessinger got on the phone to talk to his secretary. In five minutes, Eighty-eight and Noel the Coward joined us.

"Hey, you're the dude that was in the Slurp Shoppe," said Eighty-eight, pumping Tokab's hand in greeting.

"You look a lot better now than with that hot dog stuck in your throat," added Noel the Coward.

I tried my best to explain the weird situation I'd gotten into. Before I'd finished, both Eighty-eight and Noel were staring at Tokab, their eyes wide and round.

"You . . . you're a king, huh?" Noel mumbled.

"I am indeed," Tokab answered. Then the king began to giggle as Eighty-eight flopped to his knees and touched his head to the floor.

"That's totally unnecessary," Tokab went on. "If you are Tim's friends, I hope you will be my friends, too."

"Friends with a king!" gasped Eighty-eight. "Crazy!"

We started our tour by dropping in on a couple of classes. In each one the students gawked, especially at Fez, who had to bend down just to get through the door to the room. In one senior math class, Tokab picked up a piece of chalk and corrected an equation the teacher, Mr. Hartwick, had made a mistake with. I loved it.

"I noticed," Tokab told me as we headed for

the gym, "that in each room, some students were whispering among themselves even while the teacher was speaking. This would never happen in Mokobway. The offender would be whipped severely. To go to school there is an honor and a privilege. It should not be abused."

"Many students in our country have a somewhat different notion of school," said Dr. Bessinger.

Down in the gym, a couple of guys were lifting weights at one end while a two-on-two basketball game went on at the other. Deke Michaels, the strongest kid in school, was lying on his back on a steel bench, pumping a barbell up and down with both hands.

"Two hundred and ten pounds," said Deke, catching sight of me out of the corner of his eye. "I can lift it twenty-five times before I have to rest. How's that for power?"

Before I could answer, Fez stepped forward, gripped the barbell in one hand, and tore it out of Deke's grasp. The huge bodyguard held the barbell at arm's length as if it were as light as a pencil. He tossed it into the air a couple of times and finished up by twirling it about like a drum major's baton. Then he handed it back to Deke, who groaned as he took the weight.

"How's *that* for power, Deke?" I asked.

Out on the athletic field a baseball game was going on. I gave Tokab a quick explanation of the game.

"So, the . . . the pitcher throws the ball, and the batsman attempts to strike it," said the king. "But why then does the pitcher throw so fast? Wouldn't the ball be easier to hit if . . ."

"The pitcher and the batter are on different sides, Tokab," I replied.

"I see, I see. Then the pitcher must hurl the ball in such a way that it becomes difficult to hit. Timmy?"

"Yeah, Tokab?"

"Would Fez be permitted to make a throw?"

"Sure. Why not?" I got Dr. Bessinger to stop the game and told him what Tokab wanted. The bodyguard lurched toward the mound and took the ball from the awed pitcher, who stared up at him wide-eyed.

Fez examined the ball and rubbed it with his fingers as if it were a marble he'd found. Behind the plate the catcher held up his mitt as a target. "Come on, big guy!" he hooted. "Put 'er right here."

Suddenly, with no windup, Fez snapped his arm forward. He had to have thrown the ball, but nobody saw it. Certainly not the batter, who stood with the bat on his shoulder, still waiting for the pitch.

WHAP! The ball socked loudly into the pocket of the catcher's mitt, and the catcher let out a howl of pain.

"Nobody can pitch that fast," said Noel the Coward in an awed voice. "Not here, not in the big leagues—nowhere."

"It is a gift Fez has," said Tokab with a smile. "As a child he fed his family by bringing down small animals with stones he threw at them. He never misses."

I couldn't help wondering what would happen if Fez decided to fling a rock at my head. How were all those guards going to stop something like that?

Back in the principal's office, Dr. Bessinger asked Tokab how he'd enjoyed his tour.

"Most interesting," said the king. "Particularly the concept of both young men and young women being educated together. In my country, girls learn only those things which will allow them to serve their husbands more efficiently."

I just hoped Tokab wouldn't start talking that way in front of my sister. She'd take him apart— if Fez didn't get to her first.

"Now then," said Dr. Bessinger, rubbing his hands together, "what else can I do for your majesty?"

I had a thought. If I was going to risk my life to be Tokab's buddy, I might as well get a little fun out of it, too. I whispered in his ear, and then he turned to the principal.

"I should be most grateful," said Tokab, "if Tim's companions, Mr. Perry Ruswell and Mr. Noel Feeney, could be dismissed from school so they might accompany me for the remainder of the day."

I mean, what are friends for if you can't do 'em a favor when you get the chance? Dr. Bessinger scowled and looked at me with eyes that were like flamethrowers. But what could he do? The king had spoken.

"What a day!" I heard Eighty-eight whisper to Noel the Coward. "We're goin' out and play!"

So that afternoon the four of us—Tokab, Eighty-eight, Noel the Coward, and I—rode our bikes into town. From somewhere, Arlo Dexter had found a bike for Tokab that was even better than my new Rushwind.

Our jaunt wasn't quite as carefree as it sounds, though. We had one of those big limousines in front of us and another one behind. Each one was filled with Mr. Coffin's agents, ready to pounce on anybody who even coughed in our direction. That was fine with me, because Fez was also in the rear car.

Eighty-eight wanted to go to Peckham's Music Emporium first. He headed straight for the record department.

Tokab was fascinated by all the instruments. He especially liked the electric organ. He kept fiddling with the keys, making sounds like elephants with the bellyache.

"In Mokobway, only the very wealthy could afford such a thing," he said.

We left the store and pedaled along Main Street. Tokab couldn't get over all the cars parked at the curb. "There are but three automobiles in all of Mokobway," he told us. "I own them all."

The Green Garden had a display of power mowers out in front, next to bags of Gro-Kwik lawn food. Tokab asked about the bags.

"You put that stuff on the grass, and it grows faster," I told him.

"And the machines there?"

"You use them to cut the grass down so it doesn't get too long. Just about everybody in town owns one."

"People buy the powder in the bag to make grass grow," said Tokab with a frown. "Then, when it's growing nicely, they buy a machine to cut the grass down. And the grass they cut—is it fed to their beasts?"

"No, they just leave it on the lawn. Oh, some of 'em rake up the grass. That's what those bags in the corner are for. Then they put it on the curb for the trash collectors."

"What you're telling me is that they pay to make the grass grow so they can pay again to cut it and then pay yet another time so someone will take it away. Strange—very strange."

It *did* sound strange, the way Tokab put it.

We did the whole town, and Tokab was fascinated with everything. At the police station he couldn't find whips or branding irons or anything to make criminals confess, and he decided that in America such necessary instruments were kept hidden so honest people wouldn't be upset by them.

By the end of the day, Eighty-eight and Noel the Coward still couldn't get over the idea that Tokab was a king. "So long, your kingness," said Eighty-eight. "I gotta get home and tell Mom where I've been all day. Then she'll make me do the supper dishes, because she'll be sure I'm lying to her."

Noel the Coward, looking over his shoulder at the king as he headed for home, ran his bike smack into a maple tree.

"Tomorrow, Tim," said Tokab as we pedaled toward Wycliff Crescent, "we will play at the golf. I hope it will give me as great enjoyment as I have experienced today."

·5·

Second Attempt

Early Wednesday morning, just after Laura left for school, I was wakened by the ringing of our telephone. Groggy with sleep, I fumbled with the receiver and put it to my ear. "H'lo," I mumbled.

"Timmy? It's Mother."

Suddenly I was wide awake. Could she and Dad be coming home early? That'd be all I needed.

"Hi, Mom. What's the problem?"

"Nothing, dear. It's still the middle of the night here in California, but I couldn't sleep for worrying about you and Laura. So I had to call before you left for school. How's everything going there?"

Just dandy, I thought to myself. I saved the life of a king, and now I'm his best friend as well as being a government agent. I almost got run down by a car, and I may end up dead yet if the king's bodyguard gets another chance at me. Today I won't be in school because the king and I are playing golf.

Of course, I couldn't tell Mom any of that.

"Everything's calm and peaceful," I told her. "Kind of boring, as a matter of fact. Laura's gone, and I was just leaving. Another minute, and you'd have missed me."

"You and Laura haven't been fighting, have you?"

"Mom, how could you even think of such a thing?"

"Well, you two be good, and maybe we'll bring you a present when we come home."

"I'd like to talk, Mom. But I gotta run, or I'll be late for school. 'Bye."

A present? I thought as I quickly hung up the phone and got dressed. There was another problem I had. How was I going to explain my new bike to my parents? Before I had time to worry much about it, I heard a horn beep outside. It was Arlo, driving one of those long limousines. I grabbed my golf clubs and headed for the door.

Right then, I needed a good laugh. I got it when Arlo opened the car's front door and I spotted Elo.

The fat little prime minister had on plus fours—those baggy golf pants that come tight at the knee—and long socks that were bright red. His sweater didn't come all the way down over his big belly, and below it was a strip of green shirt and a wide belt with that beeper box hanging from it. He looked like something out of a cartoon.

In the backseat, Tokab was sitting between Fez and Jacob Coffin. I gave my clubs to Arlo to stick in the trunk and squeezed in beside Elo. As soon as I slammed the door, two other cars full of agents took positions behind and ahead of us. We were off.

"We'll be playing at Kemper Bay Club, Tim," said Arlo. "Is that okay with you?"

Okay? Kemper Bay was a private club on the North Shore, so exclusive that if your ancestors hadn't come over on the *Mayflower*, you didn't have a chance of joining. All my life I'd wanted to play there, and now I was going to. But somehow I wasn't as thrilled as I expected to be.

I kept wondering if the car that had chased me

Monday night had really been a coincidence, the way Coffin thought. Or was somebody out to . . .

The Kemper Bay Clubhouse was an ornate wooden building, freshly painted and with a flag above it that snapped in the breeze. "Take careful notes of all this, Elo," ordered Tokab as we glided to a stop at the huge front door. "If I enjoy this game, we may wish to construct something similar in Mokobway."

In the front seat next to Arlo, the prime minister began writing busily in that notebook of his. I wondered how many of those things he'd filled, in just the past few days.

While Fez took our golf bags out of the trunk, and Tokab ambled off to inspect the first tee, Elo said something about contacting his embassy to check for messages. He and Arlo went looking for a telephone. Coffin and I remained standing beside the limousine.

"Mr. Coffin," I said. "Now that we're alone, I've got something that needs saying. It's all very nice to be out of school and playing golf here at Kemper Bay and all that. But I think you ought to know, this agent stuff's got me scared. I really don't want to die, even if my killer does think

I'm somebody else."

"We'll give you the best protection we can, Tim."

"But you can't guarantee that . . ."

Coffin shook his head. "For what it's worth, I don't think you're running much risk. You shouldn't take that car business too seriously. And if it's any satisfaction, you're doing your government—and your country—a great service."

"You may not like hearing it, Mr. Coffin, but that's not why I'm doing all this. And it's not to get out of school or have a little excitement, either. To tell the truth, when I was being chased by that car, I had enough excitement to last me the rest of my life."

"Then why . . ."

"You said I was to make friends with Tokab. Well, your plan worked, better'n you know. I really like Tokab, and not just because he's a king, either. He's my buddy—a real pal."

"That's great, Tim. Just what we wanted. But why are you telling me all this now?"

"I just think you should know that from now on, I'm not interested in what you or the government thinks, and I don't care about a big pool of oil under some nation I never heard of a week ago. All I want is to try and make sure nothing happens to my friend Tokab."

Coffin thought about this for a minute or so. "Quilt," he said finally, "if you were one of my regular agents, I'd fire you on the spot for letting friendship interfere with your job. Still, I can't help wishing I had a friend like you."

I shook my head and turned to go. "No way, Mr. Coffin. I don't really like your line of work."

We walked toward the first tee. Arlo had three golf carts lined up. I took one, Tokab and Fez paired off at another, and Elo had the third. He was so fat he took up the whole seat.

I saw Arlo and his agents move out to stand behind trees and bushes where they could keep an eye on us without being conspicuous.

I explained to Elo and Tokab that the object was to get the ball in the hole in the least number of strokes, and then gave the king a quick lesson in how to swing. "You go first, Tim," he said. "Let me see how you do."

I got a respectable drive—about two hundred yards, with only a slight fade—and then Elo stepped up to the tee. He took a swing that looked like he was bashing a snake with a club, and the ball dribbled off into the rough.

"The game is not as easy as you make it look, Tim," said Tokab as he teed up his ball.

The king swung . . . and missed the ball. He tried again, with the same result. The third time, he just brushed the ball, and it rolled about five feet down off the tee.

Angrily, Tokab threw down his club and muttered something in his native language. I had a pretty good idea, though, what he was saying, and I was glad my sister wasn't there to hear it.

"Fez!" he snapped, picking up the club. "You do it!"

"Yes, Majesty," said Fez in that foghorn voice. He took the club from Tokab, replaced the ball on the tee and got ready to swing. Being so tall, he had to bend way over just to get that club to ground level. He looked really awkward, and I couldn't wait to see him make a fool of himself. Try and run me down, you big goon, I thought. Well, now, let's see how you do when . . .

SWISH . . . CLICK . . . The ball started off straight, but only a few feet above the ground. I figured it'd drop about a hundred yards out. Not a bad drive for a first try. Not as good as mine, of course. Only . . .

Instead of coming down, the ball started rising. Up it went, and out. And straight at the pin.

It finally came down at the edge of the green, nearly three hundred sixty yards away. Jack Nicklaus couldn't hit one that far or that straight on the best day he ever had.

Was there *anything* that Fez couldn't do? Okay, Tokab four-putted, and I got a par, so I won the hole. Big deal. That great drive of Fez's was what wowed all those rich guys on the porch of the clubhouse.

Elo? He scored a seventeen. That didn't include the times he kicked the ball out of the rough either.

That's the way most of the round went. Fez would drive the ball, and then Tokab played the rest of the hole. It didn't seem fair somehow. I'd been planning on doing a little showing off for Tokab, but his bodyguard was having all the really great shots. It wasn't until the fifteenth hole that I got my revenge.

The fifteenth is a short par three, only about a hundred and thirty yards long. I could have said something about how to play it, but I decided to keep my mouth shut and let Fez do his thing.

Sure enough, he stepped up to the ball with his drive, and *WHAM.* His usual three-hundred-and-fifty-yard drive. It went over the hole, across the beach, and landed somewhere out in the ocean. I was too polite—and scared—to laugh at Fez, so I just kind of snickered behind my hand.

The sixteenth, though, was where things got deadly—and I mean *deadly*. It's a long par four, with woods all around. Behind the green the ground drops steeply into a sand trap. That trap is where my second shot landed.

Tokab, who was on the green with Fez, watched to see how I'd get out of the sand. I grabbed my pitching wedge, kind of took aim, and hauled back for my shot. My club was still over my shoulder and I was ready to send it smashing down, when . . .

THUNK. A blast of sand shot up into my eyes, and the ball jumped out of the trap and onto the green—*all by itself!* I looked up in amazement, just in time to see Fez staring at my ball as if he thought it'd bite him. Then, real quick, he reached down into the sand trap, yanked me out, and tucked me under one arm. Running to Tokab, he pushed the king to the ground, threw me beside him, and slammed that huge body on top of us both.

I tried to scream for help, but my mouth was full of grass. I couldn't breathe. I was going to die. Fez was murdering me, right out there in the open.

I heard Tokab shout an order, and suddenly Fez rolled off. Saved in the nick of time! I turned my head to the side and gasped for air. Then I opened one eye.

Tokab and Elo both lay flat on the ground. "What's going on?" I gurgled, spitting grass from my mouth. Fez jerked his hand, and something rolled in front of my nose.

It was my golf ball. But now one side of it was torn open as if a bite had been taken out of it. A spaghettilike mass of rubber bands stuck out of the opening, and a sticky fluid from the center oozed into my palm.

"Someone fired a shot," rumbled Fez. "It hit the golf ball."

"Shot? I didn't hear any . . ."

"Undoubtedly the gun had a silencer attached," whispered Elo, who crouched behind a bush. "We are in grave danger here."

I looked about fearfully and then sneaked a peek down the fairway. I was just in time to see Arlo Dexter come bursting out of the woods about a hundred yards away, running toward us and waving his arms.

"Are you all right?" he bellowed. "Did that bullet hit anybody?"

"We . . . we're all okay," I called. I was ignoring the grass between my teeth, the butterflies that seemed to be doing a barn dance down in my stomach, and the knowledge that out there in the woods was somebody trying to kill us.

Arlo reached the green, walked across it, and stared down at us. "You're safe now," he said. "I've got my men searching those trees. We'll find the guy, for sure."

I don't have to tell you, I guess, that that was the end of our golf game. To make matters worse, the government men didn't find a trace of whoever had done the shooting. One of Arlo's men drove me back to Wycliff Crescent. Riding in the backseat, all by myself, I had all I could do to keep from bawling.

As soon as I got home I grabbed the phone and punched in SIS-BOOM-BAH. My hand was trembling so much, it took me three tries. The phone rang about nine times and then a woman's voice answered.

"Mr. Coffin's office."

"Th-th-this is Timothy Quilt. And I want to talk to Mr. Coffin."

"I'm very sorry, Mr. Quilt." Her voice reminded me of somebody slathering mayonnaise on soft bread. "Mr. Coffin won't be available for the rest of the day. Can I take a message?"

"No . . . I mean, yeah. Just tell him that I quit!"

Apparently Jacob Coffin wasn't quite as busy as the woman made out. He was at our front door within fifteen minutes, and he had Arlo Dexter with him. When I opened the door, the two of 'em were arguing.

"You had enough men out on that golf course to protect an army!" Coffin hissed, trying to keep his voice down and at the same time show Dexter how mad he was. "How could anybody sneak in and . . ."

"Chief, I had 'em deployed just like we learned in training." Arlo had a look on his face like a whipped puppy. "I kept walking around and checking up. But I didn't see . . . Oh, hi, Tim."

Coffin and Dexter entered the house and sat down on the sofa. Dexter kind of hung his head in shame and let Coffin do all the talking.

"Scared, aren't you, Tim?" he said.

"You bet I'm scared. Wouldn't you be? Monday evening I'm almost run down by a car, and now somebody takes a shot at me. I want out, Mr. Coffin. Oh . . . You . . . Tee—Out! When I signed on to be King Tokab's buddy, I didn't bargain for anything like this. It's not a big adventure like the James Bond movies anymore. I could have been killed out there!"

"I don't suppose it'd be any use to remind you it's Tokab himself that guy was trying to hit. A gun with a silencer isn't all that accurate."

"Oh, that's just peachy!" I squeaked sarcastically. "So I'm just supposed to say, 'Go away, bullet, and hit the king instead.' If I'm dead, what good will it do me to find out it was just another mistake?"

"Yeah, you're right." Coffin stared at the floor for a long time in silence. "I wish I could figure out who's behind all this," he said finally.

"I'd bet my new bike it's that bodyguard, Fez," I told him.

"The way I understand it," said Coffin, "Fez did his best to protect you and Tokab."

"Yeah, sure. He had to make it look that way, once the shot missed. But I'll bet he's got other people working for him, just the way you SIS-BOOM-BAH guys have. Fez gets Tokab and me to a certain spot on the golf course, and he has somebody else hiding in the trees, and . . . BANG!"

Then another thought popped into my head.

"First the car . . . now the shot. . . . Hey! Maybe Fez and his men aren't after Tokab at all. Maybe *I'm* the one they want to hit."

"But why would Fez want to murder you?" Arlo asked.

"I don't know. Maybe he hates my being friends with Tokab. Maybe a lot of things. But twice now, I've just missed being killed. And Fez always looks like he hates my guts. And he's big and ugly and . . ."

"If Fez frightens you, we could order him home, I guess," said Coffin. "But that'd make Tokab mad, and he'd go, too. What a mess this is."

"But it's your mess, Mr. Coffin. I just want to get out of it."

For a long time, Coffin seemed to be thinking things over. Finally he looked me straight in the eye.

"Tim? D'you remember that talk we had earlier—about how Tokab and you are buddies?"

"Yeah," I said grudgingly.

"Let's just suppose for a minute that it *is* Tokab these assassins are after. How would you feel reading in next week's newspaper that your buddy'd been murdered, and knowing you might have been able to do something to prevent it?"

I stared at Coffin and wrinkled my nose as if I smelled something real bad. "That's a pretty lousy thing to lay on my plate, Coffin," I sneered. "You stink."

He just shrugged. "We need you, Tim. Just a little longer. You'd be doing your country a tremendous service. I'd be grateful—"

"What makes you think I want your—"

"And so would—"

Just then, Arlo looked over at Coffin with a shocked expression. Coffin stopped talking as fast as if he'd had his throat cut.

"So would . . . who?" I asked.

"Noth-nothing. Just forget I said anything," Coffin told me. "If you want to quit—and you have every right to—then go ahead and quit."

"Wait a minute," I protested. "Just now, you wanted something—for me to go on being pals with King Tokab. Now it's my turn to want. And what I want is to know what's really going on here. So who's this person who'd be so grateful for my services?"

For what seemed like forever, Coffin and Arlo

stared at each other. "I guess we'll have to tell him," Coffin said finally, "if it's the only way he'll stay on the job."

"Well, it's your neck, not mine," Arlo replied.

Coffin turned to face me. "Quilt, if you let one word of what I'm about to say get outside this room, I'll have you locked up and throw away the key. Understood?"

"Yes . . . yes, sir."

"On Friday—just two days from now—the President of the United States will be here in Maconville!"

"The president! But . . ."

"Shhhh." Coffin put a finger to his lips. "It's a secret. The president and Tokab are going to tour your village—a typical American town. No big parade or anything like that. Tokab and the president will just drive around for an hour or so, and then they'll take off for New York City and the U.N., where the king'll give his speech."

"But if the president comes here, people will want to see . . ."

"The whole idea, Tim, is for nobody to know anything about the visit beforehand. That way, it'll be a lot less dangerous for the president, as well as Tokab himself."

"But what's this got to do with me?" I asked.

"Somehow, Tim, SIS-BOOM-BAH has got to keep Tokab safe until the president arrives on Friday. Besides being the king's friend, you know Maconville better than I or any of my men. You're aware of the places Tokab should stay away from, and you can steer him around without his getting sore at you. You're the perfect one to spot a dangerous situation before it gets out of control. Don't you think Tokab deserves your friendship—and your protection—a little while longer?"

This was more than I'd ever bargained for when I'd agreed to join SIS-BOOM-BAH. My mind was whirling as I tried to figure out what to do.

"Just a couple more days, Tim," Coffin pleaded. "Please. Tomorrow, the king wants to visit a shopping mall. With all those people around, nobody'd dare try anything. And my men'll stick closer to you than a coat of paint. We'll do everything we can to keep you safe. I swear it. In return, the government will give you anything you want. A ride in the president's private plane. An appointment to one of the military academies. Just name it, and you've got it."

"Can you promise I'll never have my income

tax returns audited as long as I live?" I asked. "Dad had it happen once and he said it was worse than having a tooth pulled."

"Hmmm. I dunno. Those tax guys are really tough. Even the president . . . Look, I don't guarantee, but I'll do my best. Okay?"

"No."

Coffin's face fell. "Well, if you don't want to . . ."

"Forget what the government can do for me, Mr. Coffin. Didn't you listen to me this morning? If I decide to help out, it'll be for Tokab. He's my buddy."

"Then you'll . . . ?"

I nodded.

"And you won't tell anybody about the president coming here?" asked Arlo. "It's important for the safety of both the president and King Tokab that nobody find out in advance."

"Okay," I said.

An hour or so after Coffin and Dexter left, Laura came busting in from school. Bad day. She'd missed getting elected treasurer of the student council by thirty-four votes, and she and Ralph Dean had had a fight.

"And just what happened to *you* today while

I was in school?" she asked with a sneer. "Did you have just a grand old time with King Tokab?"

"Nothing happened, Laura," I mumbled. "Nothing at all."

·6·

Good-bye,
My Brother

To my sister Laura, shopping is right up there with food and water as one of the necessities of life. So when she found out on Thursday that Tokab and I would be spending the day at the Roosevelt Field Shopping Mall while she was in school, she about threw a fit.

"You'll be in all those stores," she screeched, jamming papers into her book bag. "And with a *king*! While I'm cutting a frog apart in biology. Couldn't you at least have asked if I could come along, mallet brain?"

"Sorry, Sis," I chuckled, not feeling sorry at all. "It'll be rough on me, but somebody's got to do it." I love it when Laura gets sore that way. But there was another reason I was glad she wouldn't be with us. I hadn't told her about being shot at on the golf course, and the chance of her getting hurt was something I didn't want to have to worry about.

About an hour after Laura left for school—still griping and moaning—the three limousines backed out of the driveway across the street. I got in the center one and sat down next to Tokab, and we were off for the mall.

Arlo pulled up to the front door of Macy's, and we all piled out of the cars. With about a dozen of us, including the SIS-BOOM-BAH men all standing around, we had a little trouble deciding who'd go through the revolving doors first, but finally we all got inside. There in front of us was a big display of women's underwear and nightgowns.

Why is it that whenever you enter a department store, the first thing you see is stuff like nightgowns? Why can't they have something neat like golf clubs or model cars or records?

I tried to hurry us along to the rest of the mall, but Tokab seemed to be in a daze. He stared at the counters filled with cameras and perfumes and jewelry and shoes as if he couldn't believe his eyes.

"It is like a wonderland!" he gasped. "So many

glorious things to buy."

"You ain't seen nothing yet," I told him. We walked through Macy's and came out in the giant mall hallway. The stores stretched off into the distance, almost as far as we could see.

With a whoop of joy and excitement that echoed from the walls, Tokab suddenly began running along the hall. Fez and I took off after him, with Elo puffing along behind.

We came to an escalator, hopped aboard the side coming down, and started climbing. It took us about five minutes to reach the second floor. "Why did the stairs move away under us?" asked Tokab, mopping his face on a clean shirt he grabbed off a counter. "It seems most inefficient."

I explained how escalators work. Tokab had Elo jot something in that crammed notebook, and I wondered how long it'd be before there were escalators in the royal palace of Mokobway.

"Where is Fez?" asked Tokab suddenly. "He should be near me at all times."

We looked about. Fez was standing in front of a three-way mirror, staring at about twenty reflections of himself and scowling fiercely. Then he spun about and jabbed threateningly at a clothing dummy wearing a tuxedo.

The SIS-BOOM-BAH men crowded around us, squinting suspiciously at the shoppers, who had to be wondering what was going on. "This is intolerable," Tokab said. "Could not the guards give us some room, Mr. Dexter? That way, Tim and I could at least have the illusion that we are by ourselves in this glorious place."

Arlo spoke to his men. They moved away, glancing around at displays of pretzels and bubble lamps and trying to look inconspicuous.

Tokab smiled in satisfaction and pointed to a sweatshirt on a rack. Across the front was printed *Prisoner 45213 – Alcatraz*, and below that was a picture of a man in prison clothes with a big ball and chain.

"I want that," said Tokab. He snapped his fingers at Elo, who went to the counter to make the purchase. "I shall wear it when I meet heads of state. They will laugh, no?"

Why not? I did.

We trotted on to a toy store, where Tokab tried out a yo-yo. Then to Woolworth's for the king's first experience with bubble gum. Shoes . . . jewelry . . . books . . . pottery . . . Tokab wanted to see everything.

Besides the sweatshirt, Tokab bought some comic books, a Mickey Mouse watch, a slingshot for Fez, and a goldfish in a little bowl. "You're going to have one heckuva time getting that fish home," I said.

"Not a problem," Tokab answered. "If need be, Fez can carry it in his pocket." We both chuckled at that.

Finally, after a couple of hours, I got a hot dog and a root beer for each of us and we sat down on a bench to rest. Not far away stood Fez, surrounded by a bunch of little kids who looked up at him like he was the Empire State Building. I could see one or two of Coffin's men hanging around, too. But at least Tokab and I were as alone as we'd ever get.

"Oh, Tim, Tim," said Tokab. "Today is such a joy. For a while I am able to make believe I'm not a king, and that we are just . . . just . . ."

"Just two guys having a good time in the shopping mall," I said.

"Quite so. Look there, at Fez and those children. I believe they frighten him."

"I'm glad to know there's something that'll make him scared. Maybe one of 'em will reach up and sock him right in the knee." We both bent forward, smiling at our secret joke and spilling root beer on our shoes.

On the far side of the wide hallway, Elo was

pacing up and down, his head turning nervously. He'd glance from side to side, taking in the shoppers, Fez, and the government men. Then he'd stare over at us. But when we'd look back, he'd pretend to be inspecting a display of silverware.

"I wonder what's eating him," I said.

"Elo has become increasingly nervous and testy during our stay in your country," Tokab told me. "It is hard for me to understand. Perhaps he is overly concerned about my safety. Maybe something about the food here disagrees with him."

"Or it could be he's just turning into a fat little worrywart," I added. Tokab got a kick out of that.

Then he stuffed the last of his hot dog into his mouth, swallowed it, and sighed deeply. "I wish today could last forever," he said. "We've had such fun, you and I—along with a few dangerous adventures. I will miss you dreadfully when I return home."

The idea of the king's leaving made me sad, too. "Ah, it won't be so bad," I said, hoping Tokab wouldn't realize what a liar I was. "We can write to each other. And maybe someday I can come and visit you."

"Would you, Tim?" Tokab cried out in delight.

"Sometime soon. We'd have such fun. We could hunt and fish, and I'd show you how to play the game of *nipaki*, and play pranks on my older sister as you do with Laura, and I'd teach you . . . teach you . . ."

"Teach me what, Tokab?" I asked.

"Some small part of what you have taught me in the past few days, my good friend."

"Me? I didn't teach you anything."

"But you did, Tim. You allowed me to know your friends and to see your school and to live as you live here. I now realize that people do not need an all-powerful king controlling their destiny in order to be happy. And you taught it in the best way—by example, not the constant preaching I get from Elo and my council. I have always wished to improve the lot of my people. Now you have shown me how to go about doing it."

Tokab had gotten real serious. I didn't like it. I wanted to get back to the fun and jokes we'd been sharing. "Lighten up, Tokab," I told him. "You know, I wouldn't mind being a king. If I wanted to change something, I'd just snap my fingers and it'd happen."

"Not quite so easy as that," said Tokab with a shake of his head. "There are those in Mokobway who see change as a threat to their power and regard me as too young and inexperienced to rule them. They fear new ideas such as you have given me."

Tokab stood up suddenly. "But enough of politics. Before we leave this marvelous place, I must have one last ride on the moving stairway."

A short while later, we were heading back to Wycliff Crescent. Tokab gripped my arm.

"I do not wish to go back behind the fence just yet," he said. "Would it be permitted for me to pay you a visit for an hour or so?"

"Hey, you don't have to ask permission," I told him. "Just come on in."

He and Fez got out of the car. The bodyguard started walking toward the house.

"Does Fez have to come, too?" I asked Tokab. "I don't mind telling you I don't like being near him unless there are other people around—*lots* of other people."

"You are my friend, Tim," said Tokab, "but Fez is my protector. Prove to me that he intends to harm you, and he shall be executed. Otherwise . . ."

Prove? I couldn't prove anything. I was just scared of the guy. Watching Arlo position his men around our house made me feel a little better anyway.

We went inside. Laura had just gotten home from school and was sitting on the couch. "How did the shopping go?" she grumbled.

"Delightful," said Tokab. "But now I would like to speak with your brother privately. I would be much in your debt if you could leave us alone for a bit."

Laura stomped her foot angrily. "Why do I always have to leave just because you . . . you *men* . . . want to talk?" she complained. "It just isn't fair. How come that big goon of a bodyguard gets to stay, but I can't?"

"A good point. Perhaps Fez could assist you in some way, as long as he is somewhere nearby."

"Oh—all right. Come on, King Kong. You and I will clean the kitchen."

When Laura and Fez had left, Tokab stared at the floor, shaking his head. "This . . . this may be the last time we will see each other, Tim," he said. "That makes me sad."

"Me too, Tokab." We both got real quiet. Out in the kitchen I heard Laura snapping orders like a drill sergeant.

"Put the refrigerator down, Fez. I've finished

cleaning under it. No, that's the wrong way up. Turn it over!"

Tokab and I looked at one another and chuckled. "My bodyguard is a willing worker," he said. "But he is much more the fighter than the domestic servant."

"Let's never forget all the good times we've had," I told him.

"Yes. Like the gravied termites at dinner that nearly strangled you. I'm really sorry. I had no idea . . ."

"You don't have to apologize. They were really pretty good, if I didn't know what I was eating."

"And the visit to your school . . ."

"When Fez started spinning that barbell, I thought Deke Michaels' eyes would pop right out of his head."

"Eighty-eight and Noel the Coward. Such fine friends." Suddenly a big grin plastered itself across Tokab's face.

"Do you recall my telling you of my marriage next year?"

"Yeah."

"You must come to my wedding. And your friends, too. Perhaps even Laura, if that is your wish. Oh, it will be such fun!"

"But it'd cost a lot of money to . . ."

"You will be my guests. I will assume all expenses."

"How about school? The teachers would never let me off."

"Even if a king commanded it?"

My head was spinning. And I knew Tokab wasn't joking. He meant every word.

"And Eighty-eight can play the piano. I will have one imported especially for him. Perhaps the . . . the boogie-woogie instead of our traditional wedding march."

Now *there's* something I didn't want to miss. "You're on, Tokab," I crowed. "We'll be there."

"All right!" Tokab pounded his feet against the floor in pure pleasure. "We shall roast an entire bull in your honor."

Then he got all solemn. "It is time for me to go," he announced.

We both got up at the same time. We shook hands—the age-old symbol of friendship. "Goodbye, my brother," he said.

Then he called out an order to Fez. A crash of shattering dishes came from the kitchen. "Well at least you could have waited until you'd put the plates on the top shelf!" I heard Laura howl.

As the front door closed behind Tokab and the

scowling, gigantic Fez, I tried to follow my own advice and remember all the good times. But all I could think of was a car with bright lights trying to run me down, and a golf ball scarred by an assassin's bullet.

I wondered if I'd ever see King Tokab alive again.

That evening I was still feeling kind of blue as I stared at the lights in the house across the street. The doorbell rang, and I went to answer.

It was Jacob Coffin. "I just dropped by to say thanks, Tim," he said. "Your government wants me to convey to you how much it . . ."

Then he waved his hand impatiently. "Forget that. *I* appreciate what you did. It was a dangerous job, and I really had no business bringing in somebody as young as you are, and I'm sorry I had to do it. But for what it's worth, you done good, kid."

The way I felt, I didn't even object to his calling me "kid."

"What happens now?" I asked.

"The president'll be here in the morning. At first we planned on a big public appearance. But after those two murder attempts, the Secret Service and my office decided to cancel any advance publicity. The White House staff had a fit about that, but keeping the president alive is our first order of business. He'll be coming by helicopter, and it'll land in that parking lot by the Maconville train station. You can step right up and shake the president's hand, if you like. I'd be happy to arrange it."

A week ago, meeting the President of the United States would have been the greatest thing in the world. But now I was too sad and worried about Tokab to care. I shook my head.

"No thanks. I don't want any special favors. Just . . . just take care of Tokab."

"Sure, Tim. The president'll greet Tokab right there in the parking lot, and the two of 'em will get in a limousine Arlo Dexter will have waiting. Guards all over the place so there'll be no chance for any funny business. A quick spin around the village here, and then off to the U.N. All over. Done. The end." Coffin made a wiping motion with his hands.

"Mr. Coffin?"

"Yeah, Tim?"

"Tokab's just a boy—like me. Why would anybody want to kill him?"

"A lot of reasons. Assassinations of the kings have been happening in Mokobway for hundreds of years. Rival claims to the throne—power struggles. Why, Tokab's own father was knifed when Tokab was only three years old. I know it's sad, but it's a fact of life."

I felt tears sting my eyes. I didn't want to cry in front of Coffin, but I couldn't help it.

"Tim," said Coffin, "if you won't meet the president personally, at least let me fix it so you could see him greet Tokab. Okay?"

"Yeah . . . yeah, I'd like that."

"Just remember—not a word to anybody until after they've left town."

"I understand. And Mr. Coffin?"

"What?"

"Could you spring Eighty-eight Ruswell and Noel Feeney from school so they could watch, too? They don't have to meet the president. I just want 'em to be where they can watch."

"Sure, no problem. It's nice of you to think of your pals at a time like this."

"It's more than that."

"Oh? Then what . . . ?"

"We're all going to Tokab's wedding in Mokobway next year. So we want to make sure he gets home all right."

·7·

A Bang-up Ending

By eight o'clock on Friday morning, Jacob Coffin, Eighty-eight Ruswell, Noel the Coward Feeney, and I were in the empty office on the fifth floor—the top one—of the Bleeker Building. Coffin was perched on the edge of the desk that was the only piece of furniture in there, with a paper coffee cup in one hand and a half-eaten doughnut in the other. My pals and I were standing at the double window and looking down at the parking lot of the Maconville railroad station.

In the lot we could see Arlo Dexter's men directing all the commuters' cars away from the rows of parking spots near the station, so there'd be a big clear area for the president's helicopter to land on. They weren't having an easy job of it, either. The men and women who kept driving up would see one of the SIS-BOOM-BAH agents directing traffic, and they'd beep their horns and lean out of the window and shake their fists and call the guards all kinds of names that I was glad I couldn't hear.

"I guess my dad was right," said Noel the Coward. "He says that if you steal a commuter's money, he can handle that. Kidnap his wife and kids, an' maybe he'll be a tiny bit upset. But if you take away his parking place at the station when he's trying to catch a train to New York City, man, you're gonna have a *war* on your hands."

"It can't be helped," said Coffin through a mouthful of doughnut. "When the president arrives, we can't allow anybody to get too close. You never can tell what some nut will try."

By nine, all the commuters had left, and it was peaceful down below. The SIS-BOOM-BAH men were hanging around and trying to appear inconspicuous. With those gray suits they all wore, and the way they kept reaching into their jackets to check on their guns, they looked about as normal as Donald Duck in a horror movie. But none of the people going about their business on Main Street seemed to notice anything, so I guess they were doing their jobs right.

A few minutes later, those three big limousines from King Tokab's house came gliding up to the station. The front doors of the one in the middle opened, and Arlo Dexter and Fez got out. They opened the rear doors for Elo dar Quaman and King Tokab. All four of them stood looking up at the sky.

"The president's chopper should be coming in right this minute," said Coffin, glancing at his watch. "I hope nothing's gone wrong."

"Stay cool, man," Eighty-eight told him. "Even the President of the United States can be a few minutes late once in a while."

"Well, I don't know what more SIS-BOOM-BAH can do," said Coffin. "We've managed to keep the president's visit a secret. If word had gotten out, there'd be mobs of people down there. Last night we went over the route of Tokab's tour of the village. No bombs, no hidden guns, not even a pothole.

"This morning, the king and the president will be riding in the center limo. Just the two of 'em, with a Secret Service man driving, and guards in the front and rear cars. And all three vehicles are as bulletproof as tanks. So I guess everybody'll be safe enough."

In spite of Coffin's remark, my brain was whirring away like a windmill in a tornado. I couldn't get the idea out of my head that something was *wrong* down there in the parking lot. But why did *I* feel that way when everybody else seemed so calm? Tokab was in danger. I knew it. But I didn't know how I knew.

Yeah, sure, this all sounds crazy. I'm just telling you how I felt, standing there and looking out the window.

Down below, Elo dar Quaman hitched back his jacket and looked down at that beeper on his belt as if expecting word from his embassy as to why the president was late. At the same time, Fez turned his back to me, and I saw something sticking out of his back pocket.

It was a huge knife in a leather sheath. Among all those guards carrying guns, why did he want to tote that thing around?

James Bond . . . James Bond . . . In all those movies, he got to use a whole bunch of gimmicks and special weapons. But the parking lot wasn't a movie set—it was real life. So why did I keep thinking . . .

At that moment I heard a sound like somebody slapping his knees, real fast. The president's helicopter. It glided past our window and remained poised a moment over the parking lot. Below it, dust and papers and the neckties of the security men blew in the wash from its propeller.

It settled slowly onto the pavement, and the whirling rotors slowly stopped. Two of Coffin's men stepped forward, ready to assist the president in getting out.

That's exactly when everything came together inside my head. I *knew* what was going to happen to King Tokab. And I was the only person there who could prevent it.

"Mr. Coffin!" I screamed. "They're gonna . . . They're gonna . . ."

"Hey, take it easy, Tim," he said. "Nobody's going to do anything we haven't planned for in advance."

"But you don't understand! In just a few seconds . . ."

"Relax. SIS-BOOM-BAH and those Secret Service agents down there have all the bases covered."

There was no sense trying to get through to Coffin. He was too sure of himself. "Eighty-eight!" I cried. "Noel! Come on, let's get out of here!"

Being my friends, those two didn't ask for any explanation. If I said to get out, that was enough. We scampered out the door and started pounding down the stairs, leaving an astonished Jacob Coffin behind us.

"You . . . you two," I panted as we passed the fourth floor, "have to do something—anything—to move all those guards out of the way so I can get to King Tokab."

Third floor. "What's all this about, Tim?" gasped Eighty-eight.

"No time now to explain. Just get those guards away from the king."

Second floor. "How're we supposed to do that?" asked a puffing Noel the Coward.

"Whatever it takes." It was all I could do to keep breathing, let alone talk. "Strip off your clothes and walk around naked, if you have to. I've got to get to Tokab and protect him."

First floor. "I got an idea," wheezed Noel the Coward. "C'mon, Eighty-eight."

We burst out of the door of the Bleeker Building. I headed straight for the parking lot while Eighty-eight and Noel the Coward ran down Main Street.

Out of the corner of my eye, I saw Eighty-eight climb up on the roof of a parked car. Noel

the Coward got up there with him. Noel looked
scared stiff. But I guess he was even more scared
of what Eighty-eight and I would think of him if
he chickened out on us.

Both my pals took off their shirts and began
waving them about like flags. At the same time,
Eighty-eight let out a scream that would have
done credit to a whole army of screeching football fans.

"I am the great Alikazzabus!" he shrieked.
"And I am coming after you!" He pointed a
finger straight at one of the Secret Service men.
"And you!" he went on, pointing to another.
"And you! And you! And you!"

While Eighty-eight was shouting, Noel the
Coward began dancing up and down on the car
roof and scratching himself like a trained ape.
"This here's my pet monkey, Kong Tut!" Eighty-
eight announced at the top of his lungs. "I'm
gonna feed all you dudes to him, soon as I catch
you. Can you dig that, fancy-suits?"

Every guard in the place began moving toward that car where my pals were making idiots
of themselves for my sake. A couple of the Secret
Service men had drawn their guns, and I just
hoped and prayed there wouldn't be any shooting.

But I still had my own job to do.

A small bunch of people, including Tokab, Elo, Fez, and a couple of others, was standing near the center limousine. I threw myself into the middle of the group like the Jets quarterback plunging through the opposing line. Somebody reached out a hand to grasp my shoulder.

I turned and swung my fist at the same time. It hit the man in the chest, and he tumbled backward onto the blacktop of the parking lot. He reached out and clamped his hand onto my ankle.

"Tell 'em to let me loose!" I bawled at the tall, gray-haired man surrounded by agents with drawn guns. "If these dummies don't let me go, Tokab's gonna die!"

Imagine me—Timothy Quilt—yelling orders like that at the President of the United States!

No time to even think about that. "Run!" I screamed at Tokab. "Run away from here as fast as you can!"

Then I made a grab for the man who'd been planning to kill King Tokab. But that agent still had a viselike grip on my leg.

I missed.

Not completely. My fingers caught something that felt like a rope or strap, and I yanked at it viciously. The man moved this way and that, trying to get free. I heard a *pop* and the sound of cloth ripping.

As I clutched his belt, which had torn free in the struggle, the pants of Elo dar Quaman, prime minister of Mokobway, tumbled down to his knees and then settled about his ankles.

Then a hand like a grappling hook circled my arm, and Fez lifted me into the air, where I dangled like a hooked fish. "Leggo of me," I howled. Fez drew back his other fist. I knew if he hit me just once, my head would end up in Cleveland.

"No, Fez! Put him down! Down, I say!" Tokab stood in front of the mountainous bodyguard, pointing a finger as if it were a gun.

Slowly, reluctantly, Fez lowered me back onto the blacktop.

In all the confusion, I was the only one who saw Elo dar Quaman, still hobbled by his pants, scurry to the door of the waiting limousine. Stepping out of the pants, he threw himself inside and slammed the door. There was a loud *thunk* as he pushed a lever and all four door buttons clicked into the locked position.

"Fez, get him out of there!" Tokab commanded.

Fez took a roundhouse swing at the car's front window. His left fist smacked against the glass. The window remained as smooth and transparent as ever.

Still holding the prime minister's belt in my hands, I watched Fez. His expression went from determination to blank surprise to pure agony. His boat-horn roar of pain echoed from the nearby buildings.

"That glass is a quarter inch thick, and tempered to resist bullets," said Arlo Dexter, who'd moved up next to me. "What's this all about, Quilt? How come Mr. Coffin let you . . ."

"Never mind that right now," I barked. "First, get Elo out of that car!"

"If he doesn't unlock those doors, we'll need a blowtorch and a crowbar to open that thing up," Dexter replied. "But right now I want you to tell me . . ."

The limo's starter whirred, and then the engine roared. "I . . . I must have left the keys inside," said Dexter weakly.

The car started moving forward. "He's going to get away!" I yipped. "Stop him!"

Everything had happened so fast that SIS-BOOM-BAH and the Secret Service men were still over with Eighty-eight and Noel the Coward. The president was seated on the pavement, shaking his head, and Arlo Dexter just stood there like he was in a daze.

It was Tokab who saved the day.

"Fez!" he called. "Your knife!"

As the limousine gathered speed, Fez scooped the huge knife from his back pocket and slipped it out of its sheath. With a practiced flip, he sent the weapon hurtling after the departing car.

The knife thumped solidly into the right rear tire. There was a hiss of escaping air. The limousine staggered this way and that, like a boxer who's taken too many punches to the head, and then crashed into the stone fence at the far end of the parking lot.

An agent named Benton, one of the SIS-BOOM-BAH men who'd been chasing after Eighty-eight and Noel, came running up. "Just a couple of crazy kids pulling a prank," he said to Arlo Dexter. "But what happened here?"

Arlo quickly filled him in on the situation. "The limo's not going anywhere with its front end smashed in," he said. "But we've got to find some way of getting Quaman out of that thing."

"How?" asked Benton. "We can't shoot our way into a bulletproof car, that's for sure."

"I'll go up and see if I can get him talking,"

said Dexter. "Maybe I can convince him to unlock the door."

Dexter began walking toward the wrecked limo. As he approached, I saw the window on the driver's side slide down a couple of inches. "Mr. Quaman!" Dexter called out. "I think you should . . ."

There was a sudden *pop* about as loud as a firecracker. We all saw Dexter throw himself to the pavement. "Quaman took a shot at me!" Arlo yipped in shocked surprise.

"Mr. Dexter knows that Elo always carries a small handgun in his jacket pocket," said Tokab, who was standing beside me. "Why should he doubt my prime minister's determination to use it?"

Arlo scurried back to where the rest of us were standing, well away from the limo and directly behind it. "Give me your walkie-talkie, Benton," he ordered. "And set it to the frequency of the radio in that car. I want to talk to Quaman myself."

Benton took the radio from his pocket and yanked out its collapsible aerial. There was a hiss of static as he turned the radio on and handed it to Arlo.

"The two-way radio in the car was on when

Quaman hopped in," Dexter said to Benton. "Let's hope he didn't turn it off." Then Dexter spoke loudly into the instrument. "Elo dar Quaman, can you hear me? Come in, Quaman."

"I hear you, Mr. Dexter," came a tinny voice from the radio's speaker. "Do not try again to approach me. I will kill the next man who attempts it."

"Okay, Quaman. I guess you could do some damage, even with that little popgun you've got. But you're surrounded, and you can't escape. So I want you to—"

"Do not give me orders, Dexter!" The voice from the speaker was a shrill scream, filled with panic. "Remember, I can—"

"Now don't say another word, Quaman," said Arlo sternly. "If you come out, I'm sure we can make sense of this whole mess. You'll be all right. I guarantee it. You'll be perfectly safe. Do you understand me?"

"I understand. But how can I believe you?"

"You have my word on it—as an agent of the United States government."

Elo seemed to be thinking this over for a few seconds. "Agents of your government have lied to me before this, Mr. Arlo Dexter. I shall remain where I am until I can decide on a course of action for myself. Please, let no one come near. I am prepared to sell my life dearly if necessary."

Arlo shook his head angrily and rammed the radio into his pocket. "It's a stand-off," he said to Benton. "We've got him trapped in the car, but there's no way we can get near enough to force those doors open."

We all looked about the parking lot, trying to come up with some answer. That's when I noticed Elo's pants, with all the belt loops ripped open, lying nearby.

In all the excitement I'd forgotten I was still holding the prime minister's belt, its buckle twisted out of shape and the beeper still clipped to it.

"Arlo," I said, "give me the radio."

"Come on, Tim," he snapped. "This is no time to be collecting souvenirs."

"I don't want a souvenir. But I think I can get Elo out of that car."

"Oh sure," he muttered sarcastically. "You're going to do it after a trained agent has failed, is that it?"

"Why not let the kid try?" asked Benton. "You sure haven't been too successful up to now."

Reluctantly Arlo handed me the radio. I

switched it on. "Elo," I said into the built-in microphone, "this is Tim Quilt."

"Ah, young man," said Quaman. "In this struggle of the legitimate ruling class to keep the ignorant masses in their place, where do you stand, eh?"

"I'm not in any struggle, Elo. I just want you to unlock the door and get out of that car."

"And why, you miserable little worm, should I do for you what I've already refused to Mr. Dexter?"

"Elo, I want you to look out the back window of the car. I know you can't shoot me because the glass is bulletproof. I just want you to see what I'm holding in my hand."

Through the limo's rear window I could see Elo's head slowly rise above the seat back. I held up his belt with my right hand and pointed to the beeper box with my left.

"I'm gonna count to three, Elo," I told him. "Then I'm going to press the button on this . . . this beeper, whether you're inside there or not. Understand?"

"What kind of nonsense is this, Timothy? Why play—"

"One!"

"Do you think you can frighten me with your childish—"

"Two!"

"Wait, young sir, wait, I beg of you! The lock is not releasing and I—"

"Three!"

A lot of things began to happen at almost the same time. I heard a soft click, and then the car door flew open. Elo dar Quaman flung himself from the limousine like a rocket. He hit the pavement hard and began a crab walk to distance himself from the car, his hands and feet scraping the blacktop and his fat belly dragging.

And I mashed the button on the beeper with my thumb.

The explosion crashed against us like a great sonic tidal wave, and the rear of the limousine was jerked three feet off the ground. At the same time, all the windows, thick as they were, shattered outward, and glass whizzed through the air like razor-sharp bullets. Clouds of smoke streamed from the openings, and then, as the limo thudded heavily back down onto the pavement, the other rear tire burst open with a loud thump and the scream of escaping air.

For quite a while my ears rang from the blast, and although I could see the people around me moving their mouths, I couldn't hear them talking. Then the ringing began to fade away. The first word I recognized came from Agent Benton.

"Wow!"

I thought that was kind of a dumb remark for such a spectacular explosion.

The next person to speak was the President of the United States, who was standing right behind me.

"Wow!"

·8·

One More Surprise

My status as an agent ended as soon as Tokab and the president took off from the parking lot in one of the two remaining limousines. I had to find out about Tokab's U.N. speech from the newspaper and TV. They reported all about how he arrived half an hour late, and when he finally got to the microphones, he threw away his prepared talk in order to say what was really in his mind and heart.

It was everything Coffin—or even the president—could possibly have hoped for. Tokab told of the many things he'd learned about the U.S. in the week he'd been here and said he hoped he'd be able to use his new knowledge to make necessary reforms in his own country of Mokob-way.

I glowed with pride, and at the same time a little shiver went up my spine as I listened to Tokab's final words on the TV: "This, I hope, will be the dawn of the most cordial and friendly relations between your country and mine. And I owe all of my newfound wisdom to a young man I've known scarcely a week. This profound and courageous individual honored me with that most precious of gifts—his friendship."

That was *me* Tokab was talking about.

Coffin and I were sitting in the living room of the king's house. Arlo Dexter and his men, with nobody left to guard, were just hanging around outside, waiting for further orders.

Laura was across the street at our house, pouting in her room. It was Saturday, and she wasn't in school, so when Coffin phoned and said he wanted to see me, of course she wanted to horn in on the meeting. Coffin told her to stay home, and she took it in her usual calm, sedate manner—she started screeching like a sick baboon. It was almost worth nearly getting killed, just to hear her moaning and groaning.

When the report on Tokab ended, Coffin

switched off the TV and then flopped down in a chair opposite me. "Quilt," he said, "Arlo Dexter and I have got a ten-buck bet on. He says you knew all the time that Elo dar Quaman was behind the murder attempts. As for me, I figure you just got lucky there in the parking lot and grabbed the right guy by accident. So own up. Which one was it?"

"Sorry, Mr. Coffin. You lose. I finally sorted things out while I was looking down at the parking lot from the window of the Bleeker Building."

"You figured out something that nobody in SIS-BOOM-BAH even suspected?" he snorted. "Come on, Quilt. Be real. You can start by wiping that smirk off your face."

I tried. The smirk wouldn't budge. "Twice," I said, holding up two fingers, "I nearly got killed. First the car, and then on the golf course. Things like that really got me trying to figure out what was going on."

"Sure, kid. Sure. But Tokab was the intended—"

"No way!" I snapped. "The driver of that car was nearer to me than you are right now. And when I was in that sand trap on the golf course, Tokab was standing way off to the side. But the bullet almost hit me. What kind of assassin would make two mistakes like that? Nope, *I* was the one meant to be killed."

Coffin thought about this for a long time. "Okay," he said finally. "Let's say—just for the sake of argument, because I don't believe it for a minute—that the hit man was after you. Tell me why, smart aleck."

"That's what I kept asking myself. For quite a while, I thought Fez was the one out to get me. He never said much, and he always looked like he hated my guts. Then, Thursday at the shopping mall, Tokab told me something. At the time, I didn't see how it fit. But when I thought about it later—"

"Let's not make a big production of all this, Quilt. Just tell me what Tokab said."

"He told me there were members of his royal council in Mokobway who'd rather kill the king than put up with reforms that would make them less powerful."

"And you figured Elo was one of them, huh?"

"You got it."

"Now there," said Coffin, pointing a finger at me triumphantly, "is where your whole idiotic theory falls apart. First you say you were supposed to be the victim. Now you're telling me

Elo was after Tokab."

"You still don't get it, do you, Coffin? Before Tokab left Mokobway, where was he getting all his advice? From his prime minister, who fed the king all sorts of horror stories about how bad this country is. And if the royal party had stayed in that hotel in New York City, Elo would have had Tokab right under his thumb and continued to pump the king full of lies."

Coffin looked like he was ready to burst out laughing at me. Angrily, I plunged ahead.

"Instead, the king came to Maconville, and I saved his life. We got to be pals. I started telling him about my life and showing him around. At the same time I was putting ideas in his head about what the U.S. is really like. What did Tokab do? He had Elo write down everything so it could be used to make changes back home."

Coffin tried to interrupt, but I wouldn't let him.

"Take the dinner that first night, for example. Tokab and I got talking about how everybody in the U.S. goes to school. The king liked the idea and said so to Elo. That's why, later on, I almost got run down by the car. Elo didn't want to get rid of the king. He was after the one putting ideas into Tokab's head—me!"

"So far," said Coffin, "I figure my ten-buck bet is still pretty safe. You're still just coming up with ideas. Where's your proof?"

"How's this for proof? When that car ran into Mr. Levering's oak tree and I was lying there next to it, I heard the clang of the gate opening across the street. At almost the same time, Elo appeared beside me. He was the first one there."

"So what?"

"Elo's short and fat and gets out of breath if he runs three steps. Would he have been first? No way—unless he'd just gotten out of the car. Oh, he didn't dare pull anything with your men coming. So he pretended to take care of me."

At last Coffin seemed to be really listening. But I could see he was still far from convinced I was making sense. "What about Fez . . . ?" he mumbled.

"Fez couldn't have been in that car. When Arlo Dexter looked inside, he had to push the driver's seat *back* to get a good view. But—"

Suddenly Coffin made a sound like he'd been socked in the stomach. "If . . . if Fez had been driving, the seat would have been all the way back to begin with," he murmured.

At last, maybe Coffin and I were getting on the same wavelength.

"It does make a crazy kind of sense," he told me. "Maybe my ten bucks isn't as safe as I'd thought. Still, on the golf course, Elo was playing with you and Tokab, so he couldn't—"

"Before we start talking about the golf course, how about doing me a favor?"

"Jeez, Quilt, you can't stop right in the middle of . . ." Coffin waved his arms about like flags in a high wind. Then he let them flop into his lap. "What favor?"

"How about asking Mr. Dexter to come in here. I'd like to get a close look at what kind of weapons your full-time agents carry."

"You've been gun happy since that first day, when we met at school," said Coffin. "And no, I won't let you carry one."

"Can't I just look at it?"

"But I don't see . . . Well, okay." He went to the door and called Arlo Dexter inside.

"Show Quilt your gun, Arlo," Coffin ordered. "He wants to hold it for a minute and pretend he's one of the big boys."

Frowning, Arlo hauled a snub-nosed .32 revolver from his jacket. After flicking out the cylinder and pouring the bullets into his hand, he gave the pistol to me. I examined it for a minute and then put it on the floor.

"Is that all you carry?" I asked Dexter.

"I'm no James Bond, Tim," he said, grinning. "No strangling cords or rocket launchers in my shoes. Just my I.D. wallet, a pen and notebook, and some change. Okay?"

I put one foot onto Dexter's gun. "Mr. Coffin? D'you have a gun too?"

"Sure, Quilt. But it's the same model as Arlo's and—"

"Would you take it out please? And point it right at Mr. Dexter?"

Coffin slowly drew out his pistol, but he was looking at me like I'd suddenly grown a second head. "What kind of crazy gag are you trying to pull here, Quilt?" he rumbled.

"Tim, have you gone completely bananas?" cried Arlo at the same time.

"I want you to keep that gun pointed at the guy who was helping Elo dar Quaman to get me killed," I told Coffin. "If you don't, somebody could get hurt, and it could be me. I wouldn't like that one bit."

"C'mon, Tim," Dexter pleaded. "This is crazy. I thought you and I were friends."

"So did I," I said, "until I got to thinking things over, up there in the Bleeker Building."

"Mr. Coffin, I . . ."

Slowly Coffin turned his pistol until it pointed at Dexter's chest. "Let's be patient, Arlo," said Coffin. "I think Tim's looney too. Later on, you and I will probably have a good laugh about this whole thing. But for now, I think I'd like to hear what Quilt here has to say. Start talking, Timmy."

"When Arlo was examining the car, it seemed to me he shoved the seat back awful fast, before anybody noticed it," I said. "But maybe I just imagined it."

"You're real good at that imagining business," said Coffin. "But Arlo's a federal agent, and I think he's a pretty good one. So Tim, you'd better be real convincing."

I tried to sound as sure as I felt. "Arlo, when we arrived at the golf course, you and Elo walked off because he said he had to call his embassy to see if he had any messages."

"A perfectly natural thing to do," muttered Coffin.

"No, sir. Because if there were messages for Elo, why didn't that beeper on his belt sound off? Isn't that why he wore it?"

"Hmmm—come to think of it, I never heard that beeper all the time Elo was wearing it," said Coffin.

"Look," Dexter sputtered, "maybe it was broken, I dunno. I just helped Elo find a telephone."

"I don't think so," I said. "I think you two were cooking up the shooting at the sixteenth hole."

"Chief!" wailed Dexter. "You really don't believe . . ."

"There was supposed to be tight security at the golf course," I went on, "with agents all around. But somebody still took a shot at me. It would have been easy for you, Arlo. No trouble for you to get your hands on a silencer. And you being an agent, nobody'd look at you twice."

"Mr. Coffin, do I have to stand here and listen to all this?"

"You haven't proved anything, d'you know that, Quilt?" said Coffin. "Sure, things *could* have happened like that. But what makes you so sure they did?"

"Because all of a sudden Dexter came out of the woods about a hundred yards ahead of the green where we were," I said.

"That's where I'd been standing all the time."

"Nope," I told him, with a shake of my head. "The sand trap, where the bullet hit my ball, was *behind* the green, where you couldn't possibly spot what was happening. Oh sure, you'd have known something was up when you saw us lying on the grass, whispering to one another.

"But you yelled, *'Did that bullet hit any-body?'* Now, Arlo, tell Mr. Coffin and me how you knew, from way down the fairway, that a bullet had been fired from a silenced gun!"

The room got real quiet all of a sudden. Coffin gripped his pistol more tightly, and it never moved from the center of Dexter's chest. "Tim makes a good case," he said. "Sounds to me like you took a shot at him, Arlo, and then raced back through the woods to avoid suspicion. If you've got any other explanation for your remark about the bullet, I'd be glad to hear it right now."

"I . . . er . . ." Dexter bowed his head and stared at the rug.

"It's hard for me to think about you selling out your country after all the years we've been to-gether," said Coffin sadly. He went to the door and bellowed out an order. Two SIS-BOOM-BAH men entered, snapped handcuffs on Dex-ter's wrists, and led him away.

"Arlo could easily have stolen the car that tried to run me down, too," I told Coffin. "He was the head agent. Who'd notice if he was miss-ing for fifteen minutes or so?"

"There'll be a full investigation," said Coffin.

"Dexter had to have done this for money. Sooner or later, we'll find where he's stashed it. But what about the bomb in the president's limousine, Quilt? How'd you figure that out?"

"With Tokab getting all kinds of ideas for changing Mokobway, Elo had to do something to get rid of him before the U.N. speech. But once the president and Tokab left the parking lot, Elo'd lose contact with the king until the speech was over. So there had to be something about that limousine—but what?

"Elo'd gone looking for a phone at the golf course even though his beeper didn't sound off. But he kept wearing the thing, so it wasn't busted. Then I remembered the gadgets in all those James Bond movies, and I began wondering whether that beeper was a beeper at all. What else could it be used for?

"The only thing I could think of was a bomb— one that could be set off by a radio signal from Elo's 'beeper.' Dexter would have had plenty of time to install it since the limo was his responsibility. And blowing up both leaders would not only get rid of Tokab so Elo could seize power, but also create bad feelings between Mokobway and the U.S."

"That bombed-out limo in the railroad parking lot pretty well shows how right you were," said Coffin. "So I guess I'll owe Arlo Dexter ten dollars—if he ever gets out of prison to claim it."

"Then it's all over at last?" I asked hopefully, after Coffin had finished making at least a dozen phone calls.

"Not quite," said Coffin. "There is one more thing."

"But I don't want to be an agent anymore," I told him. "I hate—"

"You'll like this." Coffin went to the window and waved to his men outside. A moment later the front door opened.

Tokab walked inside. I couldn't believe my eyes. "I thought you'd gone!" I cried.

"I commanded that my plane wait and that I be driven here to see you one more time," he said with a happy grin. "Elo dar Quaman has confessed to everything, including his involvement with Arlo Dexter, who, sadly, placed money above patriotism. Rather than return to Mokobway, where he would surely be beheaded, my prime minister wishes to stand trial here in your country, where, perhaps, you will be more merciful."

"I . . . I wish you could stay just a little longer," I said sadly.

"So do I, Tim. But affairs of state await my approval, even though such affairs are often, as you say, the great pain in the neck. Then there is my wedding to be planned. I remind you of your promise that you and your friends will attend. I will make Noel the Coward an honorary general of my palace guard. And for the ceremony, Eighty-eight will play the boogie-woogie and the rocky roll, and you—"

Just then Laura came bursting in with a screech of joy. "Tokab, you're going to be married?" She planted a big, slushy kiss on his cheek. "Oh, I'm so happy for you!"

"How'd you get by my men, Miss Quilt?" barked Coffin.

"I just reminded them that Timmy is my brother," said Laura, poking her nose in the air, "and then I fluttered my eyelashes at them. They were very nice." She turned back to Tokab.

"It'll be such a fine ceremony. I'll send your bride a whole stack of wedding magazines. She can have a long white dress made, with scads of lace and a veil and high-heeled slippers and—"

"Laura!" I shouted. "Will you shut up and—"

"No, let her continue," said Tokab, "what she and my bride-to-be arrange is a responsibility I will not have to assume."

Laura sneered at me triumphantly. At the same time, Tokab began whispering in my ear.

"Sometime, Tim—when I am well away and need not listen to her reply—you must explain to your sister that in Mokobway, marriages of state are performed with the king and his bride standing up to their royal necks in the rather muddy palace pool."

I laughed my most wicked laugh. I'd save that little bombshell to drop on Laura when it'd do the most damage.

"Protecting my life has become something of a habit with you, Tim," Tokab said aloud, "and I should like to repay you in some small way."

"Oh, Tim!" Laura gasped. "A royal present—how wonderful!"

"Perhaps you'd enjoy having an elephant of your very own."

At that, Laura looked daggers at Tokab. "Don't you dare," she snarled. "We had a dog once, and I had to feed it and clean up after it. I won't do that for any elephant."

"You'd better scratch the elephant," I told Tokab. "There is one thing you can do, though."

"Anything, my friend."

"I want you to write a letter—in your own handwriting, and no fair having it typed—explaining everything that happened since I gave you the Heimlich maneuver in the Slurp Shoppe last week. Put your royal seal on it, and any other stamps and stuff that'll make it look official. But don't do it until you get back home. The letter's got to have a Mokobway postmark."

"Of course, Tim. It shall be as you wish. You want a . . . a souvenir of our times together, is that it?"

"Souvenir, nothing!" I protested. "You're going to address it to my mom and dad. They'll be coming home in a couple of days, and the first thing they'll do is ask what I've been up to while they were away."

"But why don't you explain it all yourself? You remember everything, don't you?"

"Sure, I do. But from me, they'd never believe it. Would *you*?"